Friday, early a.m.
The New Year, 1975

Dear Sisters All:

Hello and love from Cape Gull! Everyone here is middle-aged, closeted, monogamous, privileged, politically incorrect, and — I'm having a wonderful time. The only person who ever says FUCK is one Nina Petrovich, a writer, who, as hard as I try not to be, I'm attracted to. She has long dark Steinem-like hair and those sexy tinted aviator glasses and, I hear, a green eyeshade when she types. I think maybe she might be ripe for breaking out of the old serial monogamy box that rules all these women (and men). I'm trying to control myself, but Sappho knows I'm having a hard time of it. . .

If I don't o.d. on all this privilege, a full report on what promises to be a most fascinating evening will follow. It isn't a commune here, as we know it, but it certainly is a community. I miss you all terribly and kiss, symbolically, each and every golden, russet, black, and brown magnificence.

With love, in sisterhood,
Bettina

P.S. Tell *no* media of my whereabouts. Enough is enough — for a while.

HEAVY GILT

HEAVY GILT

DOLORES KLAICH

Naiad Press, Inc.
1988

Printed in the United States of America
First Edition

Edited by Katherine V. Forrest
Cover design by Catherine Hopkins
Typeset by Sandi Stancil

Library of Congress Cataloging-in-Publication Data

Klaich, Dolores.
    Heavy gilt / by Dolores Klaich.
        pp.   cm.
    ISBN 0-941483-25-8
    I. Title.
    PS3561.L14H44   1988
    813'.54--dc1988-22364

                                                    CIP

For Ann Stokes
and the Women's Studio on Welcome Hill

ONE

Cape Gull, January 1975

"Better take down Wonder Woman," Hilary Hope James said. "Put her in the closet."

Drusilla Marx, the recipient of this order, a gentle order, nonetheless winced. She and Hilary already had emptied their bedroom bookshelves of all incriminating matter including, good lord, a tattered copy of *The Price of Salt.* Dru reflected that even if Hilary's brother Malcolm,

1

who was arriving for a visit, should happen to poke around in their bedroom (which was extremely unlikely), and even if he were able to read the worn type on the book's spine, what could the title, so many years old now, possibly mean to him? Malcolm James, a Philadelphia attorney, undoubtedly would think *The Price of Salt*, if he gave it any thought at all, some sort of economic treatise. And a dreary one at that. It would never occur to him what meaning the title actually held. Books published these days were quite another matter. Such extraordinary candor. Dru was not at all sure how she felt about the new openness. And now, and amazingly so, her baby sister Bettina was in the midst of it all. Hilary, on the other hand, knew exactly how she felt: Guests were arriving. One planned menus, put out clean towels, and de-lesbianized. Elementary.

Dru eyed the life-sized cardboard puppet of Wonder Woman tacked up on the inside of the bedroom door. She took in the woman's strong, mostly naked body. Her glittering costume. Her no-nonsense stare. Dru stared back. Then she reached up, hesitated one brief moment, and took Wonder Woman down.

"Put her on the closet shelf, love," Hilary called from the hall as she started down the stairs. "I'll make the tea. Red Zinger?"

"Morning Thunder," Dru called back.

Tea. That meant Hilary wanted to talk. And, most assuredly, about Bettina. Whenever Hilary felt there to be a problem, she suggested tea. Talking about feelings was not something Hilary James did with ease, and tea, with its ritualistic paraphernalia, always served her well as ballast. There was no doubt in Dru's mind that her liberated kid sister Bettina, who was visiting, was, in Hilary's mind, a problem. And especially at this moment

2

when they faced the impending arrival of Hilary's brother Malcolm.

On her way to the kitchen Hilary decided to try the Winterberry. The teas, five of them, mostly herbal, with their wonderful names and wonderful packaging, had been a Christmas gift from the Lightfoot twins, Sarah and Farnsworth, who lived next door. Wonder Woman had been Bettina's gift. It had been difficult to tell who — Wonder Woman or Bettina — had been a bigger hit at Hilary and Dru's New Year's eggnog bash a week ago. Bettina, with her wild springy red hair and her bib overalls plastered with activist buttons, definitely had been an exotic presence at the annual event. Once the eggnog had done its work, several closeted women guests from Philadelphia (corporate vice-presidents all, Bettina had later claimed), in their blazers and Gucci loafers, their real gold jewelry, tons of it, and their skinny brown-papered cigarettes, hadn't been able to keep their hands off Wonder Woman. Or off Bettina. No fewer than three had ruffled her hair. Even Sarah Lightfoot, who was not at all given to such conduct, had been entranced, while Farnsworth Lightfoot, Sarah's fifty-year-old twin, had as usual stood in corners of the party sweating with shyness and turning pinkish in cheek when anyone, even old friends, had addressed a remark to him.

Dru was mostly delighted with how her chubby baby sister Bettina had turned out: outrageous, and — everyone seemed to be agreeing — rather brilliant. Bettina had come to Dru and Hilary's house to rest after the early December brouhaha over her just published book. She had stayed through the holidays, and was still about. What was it she had told the *People* magazine reporter? "It isn't because I don't think about men that I don't care for them. It's because I do think about them."

3

She had been quoting *l'amazone,* of course, but the reporter, shod in preppy loafers as he had been, could not be faulted for not recognizing that special bit of lesbian esoterica.

What better place to rest up than Cape Gull in winter, Dru thought. She and Hilary had been resting (with almost matching trust funds) in the seaside resort for eleven years. It had taken Hilary several of those first years to get used to the fact that they had chosen to live, when all was said and done, in New Jersey. But, as she always pointed out, Cape Gull was nothing like the rest of the Jersey shore. Why, in its 2.2 square miles it boasted one of the greatest concentrations of mid- and late-Victorian architecture in the country — over six hundred meticulously preserved structures.

Hilary and Dru's structure (which featured a solid copper bathtub overlaid with periwinkle blue enamel) had been built in 1865 as a gentlemen's gaming club and for years had stood as one of the town's showplaces. By 1964, when Hilary and Dru bought the house, it had fallen into boarding house ruin. They got it for a song — and almost wrecked their relationship while restoring it to its former splendor. But it had all been worth it. The Poplar House, as it was known, was once again a showplace of Cape Gull, and, as such, a major stop on the town's annual Historic House Tour.

Downstairs in the kitchen breakfast nook, which gave onto Dru and Hilary's backyard where an intricate white gazebo stood snow-filled, Hilary poured the tea.

"They say just honey in this one. Want a sip?"

Dru declined and poured milk into her Morning Thunder. Her tea was, as its name implied, an a.m. drink.

It contained caffeine. But it was Dru's favorite of the lot, even though it was now four-thirty p.m. and just about dusk. These early January days went so quickly, Dru thought, seemingly over before they'd begun.

"Now," Hilary began, "about Bettina. First — where is she?"

When Dru said that Bettina was visiting Webb Thatcher and Jay Burloff at their bookshop, Hilary protested, "But they're men."

"They're literary," Dru said. "Bettina does make exceptions. It helps that they're gay."

Hilary made a face. "There you go again. I wish you wouldn't. We don't know that Webb and Jay are homosexual. In all the years we've known them the matter has never once surfaced."

True, Dru thought. Amazingly so. But these days, Hilary's refusal to call a queer a queer was becoming more and more ludicrous. Webb Thatcher, editor of marvelously designed chapbooks crammed with male-loving-male and female-loving-female verse? Dru, emboldened by her Morning Thunder, said, "Webb and Jay are queer, Hilly. We're queer. My sister Betts is queer. Farnsworth is not, but should be. Ditto his sister Sarah. And so on."

Hilary sat in fluttery silence. Dru, using the quiet to observe her lover, thought: Well, she's still one hell of a looker.

Hilary was as tall and strikingly lean as when they'd first met. Now that her hair was graying, styled in a shoulder-length blunt cut with bangs rather like an early Garbo do, she managed to look extremely elegant, but at the same time very much like Elizabeth, their imperious afghan hound who'd got run over two summers before. The same long legs, long arms, long face, long hands. Not an ounce of fat on Hilary. She herself, on the other hand,

5

had gone to fat, old-shoe fat, almost, she hated to believe, beyond hope. She was convinced that at forty-eight it was well nigh impossible, without herculean effort, to reclaim one's firmness. Hilary, at forty-nine, had never lost hers.

Like Hilary, she too had a lot of hair, hers being bright red and curly-springy like her sister Bettina's. The fat was a result of too much food, too little exercise, and perhaps too much booze. Not that she was at all alcoholic. But she did like her drink, lately bourbon and orange juice, something she had tried for the first time two winters ago in Key West. Hilary drank only occasionally, but she did like her wine, a plethora of which rested, catalogued and dusty, in their dungeon-like cellar.

Dru leaned toward Hilary and kissed her. It was a long, wet, soft, sensual kiss. "You taste of Winterberry," she said.

Hilary, taken aback — their sex life had long since stilled to a simmer, a very pleasant simmer, but nonetheless a simmer, nothing like their first passionate years together — leaned back in her chair. "Well!" she said.

Dru smiled. "Just thinking of how handsome you are."

Hilary smiled too. And you, Dru, she thought, are still earth mama. But back to the business at hand. Wasn't it just like Dru to divert one's well thought out plan. "I want to discuss Bettina," Hilary said.

Dru, taking the initiative, said, "Ah yes. Bettina. Who would have thought that my fat baby sister would turn into Bettina K. Marx, spokesperson for us legions of American dykes?"

"*Must* you use that word? That is exactly what I am worried about. My brother and his wife arrive tomorrow

6

and here's Bettina K. Marx staying in our home. She's bound to say or do *something*. They may have even heard of her or seen her on television. And if not, we know very well that your sister is not one to keep a low profile."

"Will you stop? They'll just think that she's my queer kid sister. It doesn't necessarily run in the family you know. And she's under thirty. These days everyone under thirty is considered odd. But really, Hil, do you honestly believe that your brother Malcolm doesn't know about you? About me? About us? This is nineteen seventy-five, after all. I've already told Bettina she'll have to tone it down."

"Of course Malcolm does not know about me. And he must not. You know I rely on him to handle the estate."

"That's your first mistake."

"Now *what* does that mean?"

"Your brother is awful. A pompous, bigoted, insensitive brute. Awful. No one likes him. Even, I suspect, his own wife Maggie."

"All right, yes, Malcolm did not turn out to be a splendid human being. But he is family. And he does see to financial headaches. It's just the weekend, Dru. Then we won't see him for months. Just one weekend. Is that too much to ask?"

Hilary was seated with her back to the kitchen's bay window and thus did not see that Bettina had appeared in the backyard. In response to Bettina's nose pressed against a kitchen window pane, Dru lifted her hand to her nose and wagged her fingers at her sister.

"Dru, for goodness sake!"

Dru grinned as Bettina pounded through the kitchen door and plopped into a chair. "Tea," Bettina said. "Good. What kind this time?"

"We were just discussing you," Hilary said. "Try the Winterberry." She moved the pot to Bettina and got up to get a cup.

Hilary poured and Bettina drank. "Not bad," Bettina said. "But I prefer Red Zinger. I love that it's actually red."

Dru passed the honey. "We were discussing Malcolm's visit," she said, looking carefully at her sister.

"And how I'm going to be outrageous? Right?"

"Well, yes," Hilary said.

Bettina held Hilary's eyes and, with deep seriousness, said, "Hilary, I am your guest — and I will act accordingly. Unless —"

Hilary stiffened. "Unless?"

"Unless the prick misbehaves."

"Oh Dru," Hilary said. "I cannot have this. I simply cannot."

Dru, caught up in her sister's energy, was enjoying herself immensely. She reached to hug Hilary. "Not to worry, love. The Marx sisters will behave. We will be, what, Betts? Exemplary?"

"Darn right," Bettina said. "Promise."

Hilary, although not totally convinced, rose to the occasion. "Good. Thank you. Now then. Malcolm and Maggie will arrive tomorrow, Friday, at four. Malcolm and I will see to business. Dinner at seven-thirty. Vishnu and Govinder will cook. I've invited Webb and Jay, and the Lightfoots, and Nina and Content who will bring their houseguest, Sterling White —"

"Sterling White is *here*?" This interruption from Bettina, with gusto.

"Yes," Hilary answered, with just the right amount of nonchalance required when speaking of such a famous personage. "He arrived a few days ago for a rest. You writers all seem to need to rest a good deal. Nina Petrovich and Sterling White are old, old friends. I even suspect, perhaps, old, old lovers. Although Nina insists that she has never, ever, lain with a man."

Bettina, grinning widely, clapped her hands and said, "Brava!"

"So," Hilary continued, writing the names of her dinner guests on a pale blue note pad: "Sarah and Farnsworth Lightfoot, Webb Thatcher and Jay Burloff, Nina Petrovich and Content Beebe and Sterling White, Malcolm and Maggie James, Bettina Marx — Dru, Hilary." She paused. "Twelve. More women than men. Well, I'll serve buffet."

Good old Hilary, Dru thought. Everything planned, everything ordered.

"And remember," Hilary said to Bettina, pointing her gold Tiffany pencil directly at the young woman's "Lesbians Ignite" button.

"I know," Bettina said. "You and Dru are just good friends and I'm your friendly next door cheerleader engaged to the captain of the football team."

Hilary frowned.

Dru grinned.

Bettina, looking wistfully at her sister and her sister's lover sitting snugly in their breakfast nook with their restored gazebo in the yard beyond, thought: Do forgive them Sappho, for they know not what they do.

TWO

Friday, early a.m.
The New Year, 1975

Dear Sisters All:

    Hello and love from Cape Gull! Everyone here is middle-aged, closeted, monogamous, privileged, politically incorrect, and — I'm having a wonderful time. The only person who ever says FUCK is one Nina Petrovich, a

10

writer, who, as hard as I try not to be, I'm attracted to. She has long dark Steinem-like hair and those sexy tinted aviator glasses and, I hear, a green eyeshade when she types. I think maybe she might be ripe for breaking out of the old serial monogamy box that rules all these women (and men). I'm trying to control myself, but Sappho knows I'm having a hard time of it. I have to confess that Nina keeps pressing my latent, and not yet resolved, butch button. Needless to say, this is not a bulletin for the Movement grapevine.

As for consciousness raising, my sister Dru is a good candidate. We've begun to talk, but, because she has so many unaware years with which to deal, it's slow going. I've never really known her. I suppose I've been too young up to now. Or she too closeted. She seems to get a big kick out of me. I'm finding I really like her — and her lover, by name Hilary, Hilary Hope James, who is extremely uptight, but beautifully consistent. She is who she is, to wit, a leisured, moneyed, closeted lesbian who has exquisite taste. She works as chairperson of the town's Restoration Committee, a big volunteer job since this funny town has over six hundred Victorian edifices in need of constant care. Somehow the job is perfect: time-warped consciousness enveloping all. Despite her political incorrectness Hilary seems a very decent member of our species. I think there's hope.

Next, we have Sarah and Farnsworth Lightfoot (yes, Farnsworth), fifty-year-old twins. They live next door. They're like something out of an English country house mystery. He's shy, odd, asexual (I assume); she reminds me of my high school Latin teacher. They have tons of money. Sarah, like Dru, gets a kick out of me; she treats me like her favorite pupil. Then there are — hold on to your separatism — Webb Thatcher and Jay Burloff, who publish quietly gay and lesbian poetry and own the town bookshop. Literary clicks, you know. Last, there's this strange woman, Content Beebe, a real pill. She's Nina's (the green eyeshade's) lover. Maybe that's why I find her so strange?

Hilary is giving a dinner party tonight for her brother and his wife, Malcolm and Maggie James, who live in Philadelphia. Token straights, don't you know. I'll meet them this afternoon. Then, later, at the party, guess who I get to meet? Sterling White — yes, the S.W. Would you believe?

If I don't o.d. on all this privilege, a full report on what promises to be a most fascinating evening will follow. It isn't a commune here, as we know it, but it certainly is a community. I miss you all terribly and kiss, symbolically, each and every golden, russet, black, and brown magnificence.

> *With love, in sisterhood,*
> *Bettina*

P.S. Tell no media of my whereabouts. Enough is enough — for a while.

THREE

Malcolm and Maggie James were on the Atlantic City Expressway. Maggie was saying, "You know, Malcolm, it's extremely tacky of you to keep saying, My sister the dyke. Hilary is a lesbian. This is nineteen seventy-five, after all. It's becoming no longer a bad thing to be."

"Oh really?" Malcolm barked. "Who says? You? You thinking of taking it up?"

"Silly. Of course not. Besides, it's not something you just take up. I happen to like your sister and I also like

Drusilla. I always have a good time when we visit. And their house is gorgeous."

"Victorian prissy nonsense; fit for faggots. The whole town."

"Cape Gull is a National Landmark."

"Landmark, schlandmark."

"Well, I intend to have a good time."

In response to his wife's last remark, Malcolm James assaulted the silver Porsche's accelerator and tore into the Atlantic City Expressway's passing lane, narrowly missing the back fender of a beat-up red Toyota. The driver of the Toyota, a young woman in a bulky down parka, gave Malcolm the finger. Furious, he swerved in front of the Toyota, this time narrowly missing its front fender. Then he again stabbed the Porsche's accelerator and whooshed away — all flashing glittering silver.

During this aggressive highway act Malcolm James's blood had rushed to his cock. Since this appurtenance wasn't all that much to begin with, the emergent bulge hardly bulged at all. Nonetheless Malcolm shot a look at his wife to see if she noticed his altered state. She did not, for she had her head turned toward the Toyota — a very wide and cheery grin still lighting up her face from the sight of the Toyota driver's upraised middle finger.

FOUR

When the two p.m. bus from Philadelphia to Cape Gull pulled into its accustomed space in front of Laverne's Coffee Shop, only two passengers disembarked. One was Laverne, who had been visiting her mother in South Philly. The other was an especially large-shouldered woman of indeterminate age. This woman's India ink black hair was styled bouffant and spray-netted stiff. Her lips, which were full, were drowned in a lipstick just a shade duller than her electric orange pants suit. Draped over her shoulders was a man's Burberry raincoat that had seen better days.

This was Samantha Cake.

Webb Thatcher and Jay Burloff only had seconds to exchange looks of utter astonishment before their old friend was hugging them. Then they were in Webb's van, Webb driving, Samantha in the front seat with her cream-colored leather hatbox at her feet. Jay, who was in the back, saw that Samantha was wearing black suede pumps with stiletto heels. Around her ankle (she had crossed her legs) was a thin gold chain from which dangled a tiny heart-shaped gold charm. Jay closed his eyes and scratched in his shaggy graying beard. Regressing to his Midwestern high school patois, he mumbled inaudibly, "Shit on a goddamn stick."

Later, when they were seated before a warming fire in Webb and Jay's converted horse barn living room, drinking sherry, it was Samantha who broke through the awkward pleasantries.

"Well?" she said. "You're both so nervous I expect you to begin to squeak at any moment."

Jay, who had been sunk low in silence in an armchair, sat up so quickly his worn workboots tore at the velveteen plush of the ottoman. He growled, "What did you expect? Holy shit, Sam. Why didn't you warn us? When did you start dressing?"

Samantha was used to Jay's bluntness. And his frowns. And his growls. "It's the next step," she said, attempting casualness, "now that the hormones are beginning to take effect. It's also part of the therapy, to test the reactions of old friends and in turn to test my reaction to your reactions. Which, as they appear, and not surprisingly, are rather traumatic all round."

16

Jay sunk back in his armchair. His big black eyes, usually his best feature, were narrowed to slits. He rummaged in his beard.

Webb, tall and thin and clean shaven, dressed in wine-colored corduroys and a yellow crew neck sweater, got up from the sofa to stand near the fire. He adjusted his rimless spectacles and ran a hand through his sand-colored, sparkling clean hair. "We have to talk," he said. "It's essential that we talk this through." He and Samantha had been teenage lovers twenty years ago when they were each seventeen and Samantha was — Sam.

"Splendid," Samantha said, much relieved. She removed her earrings.

Silence.

After a while, Webb said, "Well, how do you feel?"

Jay, growling again, "You sound like a dumb Action News reporter."

"I feel wonderful," Samantha said, ignoring Jay and speaking directly to Webb. "I've never felt so well. The awful depressions are gone. They're simply gone. Of course I realize I have to watch for false euphoria. I've only been living as a woman for two months."

"Yes, I suppose," Webb said, but Jay, full of anxiety, interrupted. "How do you handle the stares? That get-up! You look like Joan Crawford used to look."

"I'm afraid, Jay," Samantha said, running her eyes over Jay's faded jeans and tatty turtleneck and the worn workboots, "you're being very insular. Not everyone dresses in counterculture fashion. At Wanamaker's or the Tall Girls' Shop I blend right in."

Webb spoke in concern, "But what if you change your mind?"

"There is no question of stopping. I'll have the operation in ten months time."

17

Jay looked at Webb. Together, as they later told each other, their stomachs dropped to their toes. Sam's new poems, which he/she had sent them last month, were solid as ever. The autobiographical content — the beginning of his/her sex change — was handled with the same skill and sensitivity as previous work of his/hers they had published. On an intellectual level both Webb and Jay had encompassed their friend's extraordinary undertaking. But they hadn't been prepared for the physical change. The few transsexuals they had come across had been rather frail looking to begin with, easily transformed into foxy young women. Except for the Adam's apple, Jay reminded. You usually can tell by the Adam's apple. But Sam, one of the gentlest of men, was also one of the hunkiest.

Yes, on an intellectual level Webb and Jay had encompassed the phenomenon. But with their good friend Sam, fast becoming Samantha, seated in their living room sipping sherry — in a goddamn ankle bracelet — the emotional content of it all was, well, as Jay later said, one heavy mother.

"What about your job?" Webb asked.

"I've been suspended," Samantha said. "But the students have rallied — some of them. We're fighting. I tried to prepare them, but the first time I appeared dressed they were stunned. I was suspended that day. We had no time to talk. They've formed a committee, the students — some of them. We meet in my apartment. Chances are fifty-fifty I'll be reinstated. But . . . I've had to get an unlisted phone."

"Shall we switch to Scotch?" Jay got up and started for the kitchen. The others said they would stick to sherry.

18

Webb, who had been listening to Samantha with great concentration, found his usual prompt anger at discrimination waffling. "I'm having a hard time, Sam, sorry," he said.

Samantha, who had been using all her efforts to stay afloat — this was the most difficult encounter so far — nodded. "But Webb," she said. "I have to ask you to call me Samantha. It's part of the therapy."

Webb, adjusting his spectacles, said he would. Then they fell silent.

Jay returned with the Scotch. "Well," he said, taking note of the silence, "if we can't handle it, old friends, who the hell can?" He had picked up Samantha's file of poems on his way back from the kitchen. Now he handed it to her. "Why don't you read a few? When reality falters, there's always poetry." He returned to his armchair.

Once Samantha began to read, all three of them rallied.

"Hilary, it's Webb."

"Webb, hello. You're *not* calling to cancel?"

"No, but I was wondering. We've a house guest, one of our poets, rather last minute."

"By all means bring him along. It's buffet."

"It's a she, Hil. Samantha Cake. She was to come tomorrow but her plans changed."

"Oh. Well then, bring *her* along."

"If it's a problem ... "

"No, no," Hilary said. "We'll be thirteen, but who's superstitious these days? But, Webb ... is she, I mean, well, you know — obvious?"

Webb, who knew of Hilary's obsessive closetedness, and realizing that she thought Samantha to be one of

19

their poets of lesbian persuasion, was quick to answer that Samantha was not at all obvious. "In fact," Webb said, "she's, well, she's quite the opposite."

"Wonderful," Hilary said. "My brother will have someone with whom to flirt."

A chill ran through Webb as he lowered the receiver. Oh my, he thought — should I be doing this?

FIVE

Malcolm and Maggie James pulled into Hilary and Dru's driveway at four p.m. as scheduled. The day had dawned sun-bright and mild. Now, with dusk approaching, it was still mild — unusual for January. Hilary and her brother immediately closeted themselves in the dowstairs library to see to family business. Dru busied herself supervising Vishnu and Govinder's food preparation. It fell to Bettina to entertain Maggie.

"Well," Maggie said to Bettina after they were seated in the parlor, each cradling a cup of tea. "I'm pleased as can be to meet you. I saw you on the Merv Griffin show you know. I've always wanted to meet a women's libber in the flesh."

Bettina winced. Here, in the flesh, in a pink sweater set, appeared to be just the sort of woman all of her feminist theorizing was supposed to liberate. Alas, Maggie also was just the sort of woman — bubbly, frilly, cutesy — she could not abide. Maggie looked rather like Doris Day — in her more bubble-headed roles — before *Love Me or Leave Me*.

Bettina cringed, but she very much wanted to avoid a confrontation. She had promised Hilary she would behave, and, for her sister Dru's sake, she wanted to keep that promise. So, trying her best, she began, "Isn't Cape Gull marvelous off season?"

"Oh yes," Maggie bubbled. "I love it. Malcolm hates it. He doesn't care that it's a National Landmark. All the Victoriana, he says, is fit only for faggots."

Uh oh, Bettina thought. She winced again. Should I? No, I shouldn't. I promised. I did promise. But . . . but. Well, just a little. "Maggie," she said, "the word faggot offends me."

"Oh? Isn't that what they call each other?"

"Yes, sometimes, but you're not one of them."

"Oh?"

Lesson number one, Bettina thought. So be it. "Maggie," she said, "it's like a black person calling another black person nigger — taking a hurtful ugliness, turning it around, and claiming it as friendly. Like me telling one of my friends what a super dyke she is. Making a pejorative an endearment."

22

"Oh," Maggie said. "Like Malcolm calling me his little cunt."

Uh oh, Bettina thought again. "Not quite," she said, her voice filled with import.

Maggie opened her very green eyes wide and looked puzzled. Genuinely so. And interested.

Bettina said nothing more. She stirred her tea. Living as she did in an all-woman New York City commune, it was rare that she spoke to an unliberated woman. She and her Movement sisters often worried that they wrote and talked mostly for and to each other. No way to spread a Movement, all agreed. Now Bettina looked at Maggie. Hard. Maggie was waiting for her to speak. Bettina decided to.

"Tell me, Maggie," she began, "why have you always wanted to meet a feminist in the flesh? And just to set the record straight, in my case it's a lesbian feminist."

"I heard you say that on television. How does your mother feel? I mean, having two queer daughters."

"The term is lesbian."

"Oh?"

"Yes. But on a first outing I don't expect you to know what is and what is not politically correct." But — Bettina silently vowed — you're sure going to know by the time this conversation is over.

SIX

Cape Gull indeed is a National Landmark. It takes its past seriously. In its heyday, the late 1800s, when it served as a summer playground for wealthy Philadelphians and similarly moneyed southern gentlefolk, great gobs of wealth went into the building of the hundreds of gingerbread behemoths that now give it its historic interest and its town-out-of-time feeling — the houses and hotels with their widow's walks and cupolas, their columned verandas and billiard rooms, their gas lighted parlors with lace curtains at the ready. One of Cape Gull's many odd features is that although in New Jersey, it is south of the Mason-Dixon line.

These days Cape Gull calls itself America's oldest seaside resort. It is at its best in summer when its population swells from five to twenty thousand and dozens of fussy, costumed events take place. In June the International Clamshell Pitching Contest is hotly contested. In July all stops are pulled out for Victorian Weekend: automobile traffic is banned, bicycles-built-for-two reign, and women with parasols, children with hoops, and men with fake moustaches stroll the wooden boardwalk along the ocean from one end of town to the other. And for eleven Augusts past, at the weekend's Antique Auto Meet, Hilary Hope James in beige duster and goggles could unfailingly be seen in her 1929 Bugatti — a two-seater touring model painted scarlet.

Winter is quite another tale. A stillness descends. Children, and not a few adults, find the place creepy. With the surf pounding relentlessly, and many of the monster houses boarded over for the winter, imperceptibly rotting from the salt spray, and the one hundred thirty-nine perfectly restored gas lights fog-shrouded, one easily could imagine Sherlock Holmes slinking around misty corners, cape aswirl in the blustery wind off the cold Atlantic.

Not that crime of any regularity has ever been a feature of Cape Gull. Situated as it is at the tip of a peninsula, surrounded by ocean and bay, there is only one road out; professional troublemakers know they easily could be trapped. Cape Gull is, in fact, a spot where a roadblock, if ever there was need, would work to perfection.

The only major crime in Cape Gull's history was, as people of the day called it, a humdinger. Its venue, forty years ago, was one of the upstairs bedrooms of what is now Hilary and Dru's house — the Poplar House — which then belonged to John Jedediah Poplar, a portly, bald Philadelphia smelter (Montana copper mines). One morning in 1935 Poplar was found in the bedroom of the house messily bludgeoned to death. At his side in the bed, also bludgeoned, was one Trixie Wildrose, a buxom, some said fat, New York City showgirl. No weapon was found. A burglar, some said. An unknown burglar. Others maintained that the deed had been done by a hit man from New York's underworld; Trixie often had been seen on the arm of a member of the Forella gang.

Perdita Babbitt Poplar, the smelter's wife, a pillar of Philadelphia society, in Cape Gull on a surprise visit, discovered the bodies in her husband's bedroom. At the time, an investigative reporter from a Philadelphia newspaper discounted both the burglary theory and the mob killing theory. It seemed to him to have been an inside job. A crime of passion. In the end, however, it was thought best by the powers that were — which included Perdita's newspaper publisher father — to leave poor Perdita in peace with her very personal tragedy. All investigations ceased.

Through the years the known facts of the Poplar Affair have been heavily embroidered. One version has it that the showgirl was really a young man — showy, but not a professional performer. It is thought that this version came about because of the sizeable gay and lesbian population that lives full time in Cape Gull and descends in droves every summer. A little shady gay history, as one Movement wit put it.

26

At the time of the murders the Lightfoot twins Sarah and Farnsworth, who lived next door to the Poplar House (and still do), were ten years old. Farnsworth's bedroom window faced that of the smelter's. When asked by the police if he had seen or heard anything, Farnsworth said he had not. Some people attribute Farnsworth Lightfoot's present day pronounced shyness, some say strangeness, to the Time of the Tragedy. Had he seen something after all? To this day, forty years later, he claims not.

"Sarah, dear, do you think I should wear a tie?" Farnsworth Lightfoot, after a hesitant knock, stood with his head poked into his twin sister's bedroom.

"That would be nice," Sarah said. She had spread three outfits on her bed and for the last ten minutes had been unable to decide.

"I think the Peruvian skirt would be nice," Farnsworth offered.

"Yes, perhaps," she said.

"Which tie?" Farnsworth asked, opening the door wide and showing three.

"Oh, the blue flowers."

"Yes. I think so too. Hilary has always admired this particular tie."

Farnsworth let the other neckties drop where he stood. An old eccentricity, that, letting rejected objects drop, wherever, a habit started over forty years ago when Farnsworth was ten, not long after the detectives had come to question him. In those days there had been a houseful of servants to bend and clear. Now there was only Mrs. Locksmith, who no longer could manage the stairs, and Delilah, who came once a week.

Sarah never touched her brother's leavings; they were left for Delilah. Ten years ago, when their parents died, Mother within a month of Father, and the children were forty, Sarah had tried to talk to Farnsworth — about everything. He had not been forthcoming. For one thing, he had stressed that his droppings were of no importance. When Sarah had pressed he had become alarmingly agitated. She received much the same reaction from him when she brought up the subject of his disappearances. He was periodically gone for a full day and night, his whereabouts always left unexplained. After that abortive talk ten years ago, Sarah no longer worried when Farnsworth didn't show up, for he always did the following day.

Sister and brother Lightfoot, each fifty years old, were not in the least twin-like. Farnsworth, who was short and round and bald, had an aura that was severely retiring. Few knew that in his young years he had been an outstanding tennis player, in fact a contender. Today, he was the least aggressive of men, the antithesis of a competent athlete. He hadn't held a tennis racquet in thirty years. Sarah, in contrast, played tennis almost daily, outdoors in season and in the bubble down the shore in winter. She was one of those matter-of-fact WASP women with short-cropped gray hair who appeared to be striding around capably even when sitting down.

Deciding on the Peruvian skirt, Sarah said to Farnsworth, "I wonder what Nina Petrovich's friend Sterling White will be like."

Farnsworth reddened and said, "Like his books, I would imagine." He began to have trouble with his tie.

"Do you mean arrogant?"

"Yes, I would imagine. And terribly sophisticated."

Sarah noticed that already Farnsworth was in a sweat; he was sighing audibly. "Here, let me help," she said, taking charge of the tie. "You and Mr. White should have a good deal to say to one another, you being such a fan." But Sarah knew that these were only words. Brother Farnsworth had a difficult time talking to anyone, about anything. She could not imagine him engrossed in conversation with his idol, Sterling White. He probably would not even manage a how-do-you-do. It was only with Hilary that Farnsworth felt his ease. Somewhat. Their talk remained within well-defined boundaries, Edwardian-like boundaries. Or, Sarah chuckled to herself, tight-ass-pleasantries boundaries, as Bettina had remarked to her the other afternoon over tea. Sarah had been delighted. What a breath of fresh air that young woman was. Sarah was certain Bettina would adore her long Peruvian skirt. She was anxious for her to see it.

"I was wondering," Farnsworth said, "do you think it would be terribly rude if I were to ask Mr. White to sign some of his books? Some of the first editions?"

"It wouldn't be rude at all," Sarah said, excited at even that much assertiveness from her brother. "Authors love to sign their books. By all means take them along. I think it's a splendid idea."

In his room, Farnsworth took two of Sterling White's novels from the bookcase. They were early works, written before White's fame. From one he removed a pressed yellow rose and from the other a perfectly preserved Gloriosa Daisy. These he put in the top drawer of his bureau, under the paper lining, on top of a *Life* magazine photograph of White — bare chested and bikini clad — on the terrace of his Ibiza villa, which overlooked an emerald sea. This done, Farnsworth descended to the kitchen, where he drank two tumblers of milk and discussed the possibility of another snow with Mrs. Locksmith, who was sorting linen.

SEVEN

Nina Petrovich had just killed off, with a Brooks Brothers paisley silk scarf, victim number two, a frail young Manhattan clerk-typist. She felt the beginning of a headache, caused, she knew all too well, by the mess of extinguished cigarettes smelling badly in the giant ashtray next to her typewriter. She turned off the machine, reached to her forehead to remove a green eyeshade, and ran a hand through her long dark hair. Then she took off her tinted aviator glasses and her cowboy boots, and went to stretch on the daybed. She stayed there with closed eyes for ten minutes. Then she got up and stood on her head for three minutes. Later, as she walked to her bath anticipating a long bubble soak, her house guest Sterling White emerged from the guest room, naked.

"Oops. Sorry, love," he said, ducking partially behind the bedroom door. "Thought you were working."

"Just finished," Nina said, her eyes riveted on Sterling's exceedingly hairy left thigh. At that moment Content Beebe opened the attic door. As she stepped into the hallway she looked from Nina, barefoot in a terrycloth robe, to Sterling, resplendent in his swarthy, hairy nudity. To Content, who trusted nothing and suspected everything, the three of them — Nina, Sterling, herself — seemed to form the corners of a well-nigh perfect triangle.

"Excuse *me*," she said, retreating through the attic door.

Sterling gave Nina a look. She answered with a shrug. Then they tackled the problem of who would bathe first. After several after-yous, Sterling grinned and said, "Hold on." He went in search of a coin. Years ago Sterling and Nina had shared student quarters in Paris and had developed the ritual of coin-tossing to see who would ask the concierge to unlock the hot water tap. Sterling flipped the coin and minutes later Nina was soaking in bubbles.

Upstairs, in the attic-studio, Content Beebe pouted. Content Beebe was known far and wide for her extraordinary pouting capabilities. She was a large woman, zaftig, fortyish, who at her best looked rather like Simone Signoret: earthy, sexy. At her worst, dressed in casual jock clothing, she resembled nothing so much as a gigantic six-year-old boy, rife with baby fat.

Content and Nina had become lovers two years ago when they were each forty-three. Their relationship, which they initially had thought extraordinary, unbelievable, True Love at last, a great love of historical dimensions — and other fantasy thoughts — had of late been undergoing strain of great proportion. Nina had all but run out of patience with Content's unfounded suspicions, her pondering of every move, and thus her inability to call out: Hooray! I love you! Content, in turn, accused Nina of being too controlling. Nina kept asking Content to make up her mind, but Content kept wallowing in quicksand — one step forward, a bit of a commitment, then squish, back into the muck. Thus, at the moment, their interaction could best be described as an outlandish psychic tango, and like that exotic dance, infinitely exciting, sexy, and binding — until the music stopped.

Content was in residence in Cape Gull in Nina's house only on weekends. She lived in Philadelphia in a large apartment that was all chaos and filth and cats. Except for her studio, which was kept anal-neat and never used. For Content, once a promising young sculptor, winner of many grants, had not worked in years. Blocked in her art, blocked in her ability to love, Nina felt. Both required commitment, and quicksand was hardly a foundation for such. Nonsense, said Content to Nina, you're the one who can't love. Tango-time.

Nina, a successful writer of quite predictable mysteries through which she made her living, and a short story writer of exquisite reputation through which she cushioned her soul, conceded to being demanding and often inflexible, but to Content's accusation that she was unable to love, she answered: Who can love in quicksand? And she usually added: Who wants to play all the time?

Content was an expert player. Once, when it was scheduled that her apartment would be professionally cleaned, an undertaking that Nina estimated would take at least five days, Content never showed up to meet the cleaners. She was seen that morning at a city-wide kite-flying contest in which she had entered her own creation, a splendid electric blue box with shimmering streamers of many colors. She won the contest and appeared, kite in hand, at the tail end of that evening's Action News program. Nina, in Cape Gull, saw the program and was, as she so very often had been, torn in two; she mellowed when she saw her lover, flush-faced and smiling shyly with her winning kite, but she realized that once again when she visited Philadelphia she would have to stay in a hotel.

It was extremely difficult for Nina to play. Slowly and methodically she had carved out a professional life for herself, a comfortable life now, but she knew she had to keep on track, keep producing, for there was no family money for ballast: she had her old leftist union-organizing father to thank for that — a mixed blessing. Nina also liked to write, to see the words accumulate on the green paper, to feel the mellow tiredness once she rose from her typewriter. However, all too often through the years she had risen from her typewriter eager for play, but there had been no one about. When she met Content on a Cape Gull tennis court, within that three-day weekend they spent together she knew that she had found someone who always would be there ready to play, someone who did it with such beautiful ease, such glorious panache. Nina, entranced, fell into a pattern of denying Content's pouting, her suspicions, the quicksand. She'll change,

Nina believed. But, of course, Content hadn't. Nor had Nina.

Bathed, dressed, and both giving off delicately sensual scents of Christian Dior's *Eau Sauvage,* Nina Petrovich and Sterling White sat in Nina's living room, well into their second Negronis. Content was in the bathtub where she would remain until long after the scheduled time of their departure for Hilary's dinner party. This was the first time Sterling had met Nina's lover, and during the two days since his arrival he had cast many puzzled looks at his old friend. Now, motioning with his head of dark wavy hair in the general direction of the upstairs bathtub, he said, "Nina darling, I'm afraid that woman shatters my weary mind. For one thing, why is she always disappearing?"

Nina, who had had two years worth of explaining Content to her friends, was no longer defensive. She said simply, "That's Content."

Sterling knew that that would be that on that subject, at least for the moment. But he was concerned. He hadn't seen Nina in three years and when he first received her ecstatic air letters about how she had found, at last, at long last, True Love, he had been delighted. He himself longed for something that at least resembled love, forget the True, but it had never appeared, not since he'd realized he was gay, and certainly not in his straight years. Many times it had seemed like love (never in his straight years), but it had always slowly ebbed away. What was it Gertrude Stein had written? Things as they seem are not things as they are, or maybe it was the other way around. Well, whatever. Gertie knew many things.

And so much before anyone else. Could Nina be going through a case of seeming?

Nina was again thanking Sterling for the three bottles of *Eau Sauvage* he had picked up for her at a duty free shop. They shared so much, so many years. Once, sitting on Sterling's Ibiza terrace, looking out to sea, Sterling had said, Wouldn't it be fine if they were straight, since their relationship clicked in so many ways. But Nina had said, and Sterling had agreed, that if they were straight they wouldn't click at all in the ways in which they did click. The irony had filled them with a wistfulness that had lasted the evening through.

Nina handed Sterling the last of the cashews. She went to the hall coat tree to get coats, and called up to Content, "We're leaving. See you at Hilary's." Nina no longer cared if Content heard her and she no longer sat around chain-smoking, waiting for her lover to garner the bravery needed for an appearance. She handed Sterling his sheepskin jacket. As she did so, Sterling could not help seeing what looked to be the possibility of tears. He put his arm around her, and together, clumsy in their bulky winter coats, they edged out the front door.

EIGHT

When Nina and Sterling rang the doorbell at Hilary
and Dru's, Bettina and Maggie James were just
descending the stairs to join the party. The two of them
had talked all afternoon, moving from the parlor into the
library when Hilary and Malcolm had vacated it, then
relocating to Bettina's bedroom where Bettina had
changed into a pair of clean overalls. Maggie had not
changed for dinner, so occupied had she been with what
Bettina had been saying. At the last minute, and

completely out of character for her, she simply had added a silk scarf to her daytime outfit.

Maggie headed for the parlor to join the others as Bettina opened the front door. When she saw Nina Petrovich, her heart went papum-papum and she was struck mute.

Nina smiled. "Bettina, I'd like you to meet Sterling White."

Bettina held out her hand but her eyes stayed on Nina.

"Bettina has written an extraordinary book," Nina said to Sterling.

"Oh?" Sterling said. "A novel?"

Nina laughed. "Hardly. It's a rollicking good look at our lives and our history."

"Oh?" Sterling said. "I'd like to read it. Do you have a reading copy?" he asked Bettina.

Bettina, off in a fantasy of Nina climbing into her bed wearing nothing but a green eyeshade, did not hear what Sterling had said.

"Bettina?" Nina said. "Are you all right?"

"What? Oh. Yes. I love your work, Mr. White. I've always loved it." Bettina realized she was gushing, an ability she had not been aware she possessed. She was still looking at Nina.

Nina told Sterling that she had a copy of Bettina's book. Sterling said good. Then they stood there waiting for Bettina to usher them into the party. When she didn't Sterling said, "Well, shall we join the others?" He took Bettina's elbow and turned her toward the parlor. He whispered to Nina, "Someone's got a crush on you, darling." Nina smiled.

Jerk! Bettina said to herself after she'd deposited Nina and Sterling at the bar. You jerk! You're acting just like some teenage boy. Oh self-possessed one, you're a jerk. Right. Shape up! She walked to where her sister Dru stood near the buffet table.

"Hi," Dru said. "Have you met Samantha Cake?"

"Who?"

Dru pointed.

"Whoa . . . "

"She's a friend of Webb and Jay's. Isn't she unusual looking?"

Bettina grinned. "That's because she's a he."

"What? Whatever are you saying? Don't be ridiculous. She's wearing stiletto heels."

Bettina laughed. "Sis, you've been living in Cape Gull too long. He's obviously a transvestite or maybe a transsexual."

"Whatever are you talking about?"

"A man who dresses in women's clothes or one who is in the process of changing his gender."

"Don't be ridiculous."

"You just said that."

"You really are impossible," Dru said, laughing, and she walked over to introduce herself to Samantha.

Bettina's gaze was roaming the room for Nina when Sarah Lightfoot appeared at her side.

"Good evening," Sarah said, her bright blue eyes sparkling.

"Hi," Bettina said. "What a terrific skirt you're wearing." She realized she was very pleased to see Sarah.

"I thought you might like it. It's from Peru."

"Were you there?"

"Last year. Farnsworth and I always had wanted to see Machu Picchu. We finally just up and went. It was every bit as extraordinary as we'd heard."

"Fantastic. I've always wanted to go."

"I want to go back. I'd stay longer next trip. I do love to travel."

"Me too."

"But then there are wonders to be seen everywhere," Sarah said. "Our own wetlands, for example."

"Wetlands?"

Sarah, realizing Bettina did not know about the famous Cape Gull wetlands, proceeded to speak of them, ending by inviting Bettina to an outing. "Sunday? Shall we go Sunday? We can lunch first."

"Super," Bettina said. "I'd love to."

"Here comes Webb," Sarah said. "He's our local historian. He knows ever so much more than I do. We'll consult him so as not to miss the best routes." Webb joined them and the three of them became absorbed in tales of Jersey lore.

Across the room Malcolm James was talking with Samantha Cake. Samantha towered over him and Malcolm was thinking: That's a lot of woman. He didn't mind having to crane his neck — but what the fuck kind of name was Cake?

Malcolm was exactly the height of his wife Maggie, five foot six, but he was powerfully strong due to years of lifting weights. He talked fast, mostly out of the corner of his mouth, constantly nodding. From time to time he raised himself onto the balls of his feet and rocked back and forth as he talked. Every so often he also shrugged one shoulder or the other. In fact, it was seldom that Malcolm James stood still. Something was always moving — a hand, his head, an arm, his torso. He was just beginning what sounded to Samantha like a dirty joke when Maggie joined them. Malcolm, who had been drinking steadily and had eaten little ("Curry, feh"),

40

grabbed his wife by the nape of her neck and said to Samantha, "Have you met my little woman?"

Because Malcolm and Maggie were exactly the same height and because Maggie, since her talk with Bettina, was now listening to her husband very carefully for oppression talk, she became mightily annoyed. She frowned and wrenched herself free of his neck grip. Malcolm thought she was playing. He laughed and tried to grab her ass. She evaded him and he stumbled off balance. She held out her hand to Samantha and said, "Margaret Stone James. How do you do?"

"Hey!" Malcolm yelled at Maggie as he regained his balance. "What gives?"

"Gives?" Maggie said with utter disdain.

Bewildered, Malcolm burst out laughing. "What the crazy hell?" He again grabbed for his wife's ass, but she was ready for him. She karate-chopped his hand away, and, taking Samantha by the arm, walked off with her, leaving Malcolm standing alone.

Malcolm gulped at his drink and focused in on Jay Burloff who was talking to his lover, Webb. He made his way toward them. They looked up from their conversation just as he stumbled into their midst. Jay shuddered, but caught Malcolm under his arms. Malcolm laughed, "Good catch, guy," he said. "You still lifting weights?"

Bettina, standing alone near the bar, was watching Maggie. She looks like a big game hunter, Bettina thought, the way she's tracking and observing her husband. And she's not smiling.

Maggie walked to stand at Bettina's side. "You're right, you know," she said in a conspiratorial voice. "I've been watching him very carefully. Everything he does and says is sexist."

41

"Surely not everything," Bettina teased, knowing full well that there was no one more militant than an appendage whose consciousness had been newly raised.

"Yes, damn it, everything!"

"But he also seems to be drunk," Bettina said.

"All the more evidence," Maggie said. And she stalked off to continue her stalking.

Farnsworth Lightfoot stood near one of the bay windows, almost inside the draperies themselves, trying to work up the courage to approach Sterling White to ask him to autograph his books. They had been introduced some minutes before but their conversation had gotten nowhere, Farnsworth having been too petrified with shyness. Just as he was deciding to get the books from the hall table where he had left them and take the plunge, Samantha Cake walked to his side.

"Hello," she said. "We haven't met."

"Farnsworth Lightfoot," Farnsworth said. "I live next door."

"How convenient for you," Samantha said. "I live in Philadelphia." She held out her hand. "I'm Samantha Cake."

"Oh, yes, my sister said that you're a friend of Webb and Jay's."

"An old friend," Samantha said. "They publish my poems."

"You're a poet?"

"Yes. I teach too. At Temple. And you?"

"Oh, I don't work. My sister and I live quietly. We travel some. Not as much as Sarah would like, however. She loves to travel. I do some collecting, art. Nothing grand." Farnsworth realized that he was talking easily to Samantha. Would that he could talk thus to Sterling

White. "What do you teach?" he asked Samantha, and simultaneously thought: What a charming woman.

Samantha began to speak of her classes, and she and Farnsworth moved together to the buffet table, then settled on a love seat to eat and to continue their conversation.

Bettina was off again into her fantasy of Nina climbing into her bed. It was interrupted by the appearance of Content Beebe at the parlor doors, squeaky clean and shining from her long bath. Bettina saw Nina look at her watch and then ignore her lover's arrival. Content, shrugging, made her way to where Bettina stood.

"Hi, kid," she said, punching Bettina on the arm.

"Good evening," Bettina said, in a voice, good lord, that resembled Hilary's. Content looked like Signoret tonight, but the punch on the arm had wrecked it.

"How're you coping with the adults?" Content asked, reaching with fingers to the buffet table to pick at the remains of something cold.

Hilary, in a billowing red caftan, fluttered up. "Content, hello, don't eat that cold leftover. Come, there are hot things waiting for you in the kitchen. Whatever kept you this time? You must eat quickly. I am about to announce the treasure hunt teams."

As they went off to the kitchen, Content, pouting, gave Bettina another punch. Bettina sighed and made her way to her sister, who was talking with Webb Thatcher.

Shortly thereafter, Maggie, who had been in the kitchen talking to Hilary, who was supervising the speed with which Content ate, passed by Bettina and hissed into her ear, "Damn him! I could murder him!"

Bettina wondered if she should be concerned. There hadn't been enough time during their afternoon talk to ask Maggie how she was going to handle her newly rising consciousness. Malcolm, aside from being a shit, looked as if he was capable of violence. All those clipped movements with those short arms. Just like Norman Mailer when he stabbed one of his wives. Bettina wondered if she had opened up a hornet's nest. Had she overdone it? But during this last thought Nina Petrovich passed by looking as if she was heading for the loo. Bettina placed her concern for Maggie's emerging feminism on a back burner and followed Nina out of the parlor — visions of green eyeshades dancing in her head. She hadn't even bothered to look around for evidence of Content Beebe's presence.

When Bettina returned to the parlor (she had waited outside the bathroom door for Nina and when Nina had emerged, saying, "Next," Bettina had just smiled idiotically) Hilary was calling for attention.

"All right, everyone," Hilary was saying. "No more chatting. Time for the Treasure Hunt!"

Malcolm groaned, loud enough for everyone to hear. Maggie gave him a withering look.

"Thank goodness it is a mild evening," Hilary continued. "A little fresh air is in order. I placed the clues this afternoon." Hilary donned her reading glasses. "I put all of your names into a hat and — *voila*! The teams are as follows: Team Number One — Dru, Maggie, Bettina, and Nina." Bettina did a motionless jig. "Team Number Two — Sarah, Webb, Jay, and Samantha. And Team Number Three — Farnsworth, Sterling, Content, and Malcolm." Hilary removed her reading glasses. "I will stay here and mind the store. Hot mulled cider awaits your return. Good luck to you all!"

As people were gathering coats, Malcolm, bleary-eyed, began to tick off who at this shindig was and who was not queer. Dear sister Hilary, he began, and Dru of course.

And the slight guy in granny glasses — Webb — and that butchy-looking woman Content Beebe. Bettina? Naw. Just a leftover hippie. And not that hunky-looking Jay who lifts weights. And not that tall woman Cake. God, stiletto heels. Pipsqueak Farnsworth? Forget it. Ditto no-nonsense Sarah. Both straight arrows. So too that handsome couple Sterling White and Nina Petrovich. A fucking handsome man, that Sterling. Malcolm was glad Sterling was on his team — if there had to be a team. Shit, a fucking treasure hunt! He grabbed a beer from the bar and stumbled off to get his coat.

NINE

"Yes, Officer Schmertz. James, Malcolm James."
Hilary was in the library on the telephone. "He is my
brother. He lives in Philadelphia. Rittenhouse Square.
Yes, two t's. Yes. His wife is upstairs. Maggie — Margaret
Stone James. Well, since last night. You see, we had a
dinner party and then we had a treasure hunt. Yes. Well,
surely you know, it's a venerable parlor game. Well,
Malcolm, my brother, never returned from the hunt. Yes,
last night. Well, his wife Maggie said not to worry, he

would show up eventually. She thought he probably had gone off to a bar. Then we all went to bed. No, just my house guests. Well, there's my sister-in-law Maggie, and then there's Bettina Marx. And you know Drusilla. Yes, Marx. Bettina is Drusilla's sister. Well, Maggie lives with Malcolm in Philadelphia and Bettina lives in New York City. Yes, Maggie is still here. She's upstairs. No, certainly there was no quarrel. It was a treasure hunt, as I've told you, a parlor game . . . No, no, Officer Schmertz, as I said earlier, it's hardly a police matter. However, as I also said, I would like you to recommend a private investigator. Someone . . . well, shall we say . . . someone discreet?"

TEN

At the sound of the doorbell Hilary, who was wound up tight as a competition yo-yo, jumped from where she was sitting in the parlor and let out a sharp squawk. Maggie, who was scrunched in a corner of a sofa, pulled Hilary's mink blanket tighter around herself. Dru, in an armchair near the fireplace, looked up from *The New Yorker* and removed her reading glasses. Bettina, bowing to Hilary's earlier request, quickly removed her activist buttons (not without a twinge of conscience) from her bib overalls. Chief Schmertz had located a private investigator: "Right here in Cape Gull, would you fancy?" The four women had been waiting nervously for his arrival.

Now, at a nod from Hilary, Bettina bounded to the front door and opened it. She stared, speechless. On the doorstep stood a tall, slim woman who was running a hand through long and luxurious silver blonde hair. Bettina gulped. Faye Dunaway? Lauren Bacall young? Pat Hemenway back from the other side?

"I'm Tyler Divine," the apparition said, offering Bettina a hand.

Omigod, Bettina thought, a woman shamus. When she took the woman's hand, hers was trembling. "Come in," she managed to say, awkwardly ushering the detective into the parlor and anticipating with relish the shocked reactions of Hilary, Dru, and Maggie — which were indeed that: they stared, as stunned as Bettina had been. Dru, who had been expecting someone like Police Chief Schmertz — gentle befuddled Schmertzie — who had patrolled Cape Gull's gas-lighted streets for thirty years, wondered: Who is this? She sat up straighter in her chair and exchanged a look with Hilary, who was fluttering worse than usual.

"I'm Tyler Divine," Tyler Divine said.

Dru, Maggie, and Bettina continued to stare while Hilary introduced herself and asked for the detective's coat. As she walked to the hall closet with it she gave an approving nod to its designer label and raccoon fur lining. Well, well, she thought, a raccoon fur-lined trench coat — what have we here? When she returned to the parlor, the others were sitting in silence. Not knowing what to say or do, so unusual for her, she asked in a high thin voice, "Tea? Coffee?"

Detective Divine, who was sitting in an armchair near the fire, declined. She flipped through a notebook. Then she lifted astonishingly blue eyes and said, "I presume there's been no word from Mr. James?" As her gaze moved from woman to woman, resting a moment on each, she twice ran a hand through her silvery hair. The gesture was sensual. Dru stared, and although she normally did not pay much heed to what people wore, she found herself noting every detail of Tyler Divine — her soft gray turtleneck sweater just a shade lighter than her flannel trousers (trousers like Dietrich used to wear), several long gold chains resting on what looked like very wonderful breasts, and her hair! This woman was a dream.

Detective Divine was continuing, "Shall we begin with your names, ages, addresses — and your relationship to the missing?"

Hilary began. "I am Hilary Hope James. Malcolm is my brother. I am forty-nine. This is my house. I have lived here for eleven years."

Dru then gave her particulars, ending, "This is also my home." Detective Divine looked up from her notebook. Dru said, "Hilary and I own the house in common." Detective Divine nodded and said, "Next."

"Bettina Marx. Twenty-eight. New York City. St. Mark's Place."

"And what is your relationship to Mr. James?"

"None. I met him for the first time yesterday."

"You're visiting?"

"Yes, I'm Dru's sister."

Detective Divine moved her eyes to rest on Maggie. "And you're the missing's wife?"

"Margaret Stone James. Philadelphia. Rittenhouse Square. I'm forty-five."

Detective Divine continued writing in her notebook, frequently running a hand through her long, extravagant hair, and the others continued staring at her. Her eyes. So blue. Professionally passive, they nonetheless unnerved. She turned from her notebook and, purposefully deciding to ignore Maggie James for the moment, focused her attention on Bettina, but as she began to speak Hilary interrupted.

"Ms. Divine, excuse me, might I ask, that is, Chief Schmertz . . . I have not had the pleasure of meeting you. Or of hearing of you. Our town is quite small. Everyone usually . . . well, everyone usually knows everyone."

Detective Divine smiled — for the first time, Bettina noted. She also noted, because her attention was so riveted on the woman, a slight tremor on the detective's lips. Aha, Bettina thought, so she doesn't like personal questions. I wonder if she's lesbian and hiding it. But then Bettina always thought that any woman working in a male dominated domain was lesbian. Well, maybe not this one. She was a shamus and shamuses always had shady pasts that might cause lips to tremble.

Detective Divine was responding to Hilary's inquiry, "I've been living quietly out at the Point. I've been in town only three weeks."

"Oh?" Hilary said, all social graces. "And where did you live last?"

Detective Divine hesitated barely a moment before she said, "East Hampton."

Dru started. East Hampton? Did she know any of her and Hilary's friends on the south shore? Tillie or Fifi? Molly or Benedicta? And why did she move from one resort to another? Interesting.

"Oh, East Hampton," Hilary, oblivious, was saying. "Charming town. Such an exquisite entrance — those

51

elms, that pond. I almost settled there, you know. I am partial to resorts out of season."

Tyler Divine crossed Hilary Hope James off her suspects list, if indeed there had been foul play and thus a need for a suspects list. It was probably a marital quarrel, she was thinking. Malcolm James undoubtedly would show up before nightfall. And yet. There was a good deal of nervousness in the room. She again purposefully ignored Maggie James, turning her attention back to Bettina.

"Ms. Marx," she said, "I wonder if you would tell me what sort of man Mr. James is."

Omigod, Bettina thought. Then, waffling, she said, "Well, we only exchanged a few words. I really didn't get a handle on him." Bettina, who had always been proud of having lived her young life free of lies was now lying through her teeth. She certainly *had* gotten a handle on Malcolm James: He was a shit.

Detective Divine pressed, but her eyes were on Maggie, who was looking out a bay window. "Your first impression will do," she said to Bettina.

Bettina swallowed. "He's okay. Establishment type."

Detective Divine waited.

Dru spoke up. "He's a competent lawyer. Has a good reputation."

Hilary broke in. "My brother indeed is a competent attorney. He is quite well known in Philadelphia. His firm . . ."

"Oh for god's sake." This from Maggie, from the sofa, from under the mink blanket, her eyes still focused out the bay window. "My husband was a shit."

Detective Divine said — very carefully — "Was?"

No one seemed to breathe.

52

"Was, is, what does it matter? Who's got a cigarette?" Maggie turned her attention back to the room.

Dru went to sit next to Maggie and gave her a cigarette and a light. Maggie inhaled deeply.

Dru was puzzled. Bubbly Maggie, always smiling, always putting a sunny face on things, her Doris Day face. Now she had metamorphosed, overnight it seemed, into Ingrid Thulin: dour, deep, Nordic. Strange. Very strange.

Bettina was not puzzled. But she was beginning to become concerned. Had she, after all, gone too far yesterday? Had her talk with Maggie led to — what? Surely not murder! Surely bubbly Maggie had not bumped off shitty Malcolm! Holy mother of dykedom!

Yipes.

Detective Divine was staring at Maggie. She decided against pressing her. Let the tension build. Perhaps there'd be another outburst. She turned to Hilary.

"Chief Schmertz mentioned the treasure hunt. Who was on Mr. James's team?"

Hilary, relieved to be asked a question she had well in hand, answered, "Sterling White and Farnsworth Lightfoot, Content Beebe — and Malcolm, of course."

"And they all returned to the party together save for the missing?"

Hilary did not respond. Detective Divine looked up from her notebook.

Bettina was uncomfortable. She was all too aware that Hilary did not want to mention the quarrel between Nina and Content (*not* as a result of her, Bettina, having followed Nina to the loo). Dru, too, had been lectured by Hilary about the need to keep everything closeted. Maggie, however, wrapped up in her own trauma, had not been a part of the morning's discussion. Now, when no one else answered, Maggie said, "Content never returned to the party."

Hilary fluttered.

Detective Divine put her pencil behind her ear, sat back in her chair and said, "Am I to understand that there are two missings?"

"No, no," Hilary said. "Content is not missing. She is in Philadelphia."

"Oh?"

"She lives there. Nina reached her this morning. Nina told me this when I rang her to ask that she and her house guests be here at one p.m. for your questioning."

"Nina?" Detective Divine asked.

"Nina Petrovich, a very fine writer . . . "

Maggie, interrupting, "It's no big mystery. Content and Nina had a quarrel and Content took off for Philadelphia last night."

Hilary blanched.

Detective Divine thought: The plot thickens. Or does it? She asked, "Did the quarrel have anything to do with Mr. James?"

"Certainly not!" Hilary said.

Detective Divine waited. In her work much could be learned in silence. She watched as Dru and Bettina exchanged glances; she saw Hilary glare at them. A full minute passed. Then Maggie flung off the mink blanket and stalked to the fireplace.

"Listen," she said. "There's no big mystery. Content and Nina did not quarrel about Malcolm. They had a lovers' quarrel. I heard it. Before the treasure hunt." She turned to Hilary and continued, "Detective Divine obviously is trying to ascertain who was the last to see Malcolm alive. Why put suspicion on Content?"

"Alive?" Detective Divine said, holding Maggie's eyes.

54

"Alive, dead, what does it matter? I'd like a drink."

Hilary went to her sister-in-law and put an arm around her. She addressed Detective Divine. "My sister-in-law is very upset. She's simply not herself. Perhaps she could lie down for a bit."

"I don't want to lie down," Maggie said. "I want a drink."

Hilary chided, "It's eleven a.m., dear."

Dru got up. "Excellent time for a bloody mary," she said. "They'll do us all a world of good. Ms. Divine? Detective Divine declined, but said she would take a cup of tea now. "Morning Thunder?" Dru said.

"I beg your pardon?"

"We also have Earl Grey."

"Fine," Detective Divine said. "Thank you."

"Coming right up," Dru said, motioning to Bettina to come and help her.

In the kitchen Bettina said, "What a fucking mess."

Dru said, "And what in the world has come over bubbly Maggie? She's a different person."

Bettina, "I know."

Dru, "You know?"

Bettina, "I *know*."

ELEVEN

Saturday, dusk
January, 1975

Dear, dear hearts!

    Where to begin? Where O where to begin? Things are
absolutely baroque.
    My last letter left you with a dinner party to come. Well,
it came all right — plenty weird, including an

old-fashioned outdoor treasure hunt (in the snow! Actually it was a mild night). And: it looks as if someone's been murdered! I kid not.

Actually, we don't know that someone's been murdered, we just assume it. There's no body, yet. And as my sister Dru keeps saying: Just like a Perry Mason mystery. You see, we all hated the deceased — if he turns out to be deceased, that is. Sexist rodent that he was (is?), I don't wish him dead. The body in question is my sister's lover's brother Malcolm James.

And, as if murder isn't enough to write home about, the private eye on the case (Hilary does not want the police involved) is this knockout silvery blonde who wears a raccoon fur-lined trench coat. There's a story there, but what it is I haven't a clue. I keep thinking she's one of us and hiding it. But since almost everyone around here is one of us and hiding it, who the fuck can figure anything out? Not I, said the spokeswoman.

The dinner party was a trip. Weirdness everywhere, including a huge hunk of a man, sweet as can be, turning into a huge hunk of a woman. He/she is Samantha Cake, a poet, a good friend of Webb and Jay, a last-minute dinner guest. I keep flashing to him/her towering over Farnsworth (the next door twin), the two of them mightily engrossed.

As for the others — Sterling White is every bit as suave as all his interviews make him out to be. He wants to read my book. Nina has read it. Called it extraordinary! Called it rollicking! I, in turn, made an utter fool of myself — gushing, stuttering, following her around like a basset hound. She was, glory of glories, on my treasure hunt team. I never left her side. I keep drifting off into fantasy: Nina, naked, climbing into my bed wearing nothing but a green eyeshade. Also, glory of glories, Nina and Content

57

(her lover, who sometimes looks like a gigantic six-year-old boy — she does, she does) had a BIG FIGHT at the party and Content fled home to Philadelphia. Wasn't around for Divine's questioning. Yes, Divine. Detective Tyler Divine. Too much, yes? Anyway, Content called me a little while ago and in this mysterious voice said she was coming back to Cape Gull and would I meet her because she had something important to tell me. Maybe she killed Malcolm (if he's dead) and is coming back to kill me because she knows about my fantasy. I agreed to meet her, pill that she is. Maybe I'll get to see Nina on her home grounds. Maybe she'll be wearing her green eyeshade. Maybe, maybe . . .

In the meantime, my sister's lover Hilary is nervous as can be, worried sick about her closeted life — as is almost everybody here. You see, most suspects in the supposed murder are either lesbian, gay men, celibates (Farnsworth and his sister Sarah, I think), or prospective transsexuals — not such a hot situation for our various Movements. The one practicing hetero in the bunch is Maggie, wife of the supposed deceased. And this brings me to the most important part of this letter. Hold onto each other: I ventured into unliberated womanhood territory with our message — feminism 101 — and, horror of horrors, it may have led to — well, murder (if there's been a murder, that is). No, no, I didn't actually pull the trigger or plunge the knife or pour the poison or hold the head under water or — HOWEVER, I may have planted, totally without malice aforethought, just such a fantasy in the murderer's head. Oy. Here's what happened . . .

TWELVE

"But you simply must tell her," Nina said.

"I know that," Sterling said, a note of petulance in his voice.

"You men with your restless cocks. Look where it's brought you this time."

"Low blow, darling."

"Sorry," Nina said. "I'm genuinely sorry. It's just that it's such a horrid mess."

"That it is," Sterling agreed, reaching for a pillow and stretching out on Nina's sofa.

He was wretched. Since returning from Hilary and Dru's, where he and Nina had taken their turns at being questioned by the estimable private eye Divine, he and Nina had been talking, Sterling waiting for the right moment to confess. During last night's treasure hunt, he and shitty Malcolm, yes, shitty, homophobic Malcolm, had segued into the dunes and made it. After which, Sterling had admitted, he had left Malcolm in the sand (near the old fort) to zip up while he, Sterling, had returned to his treasure hunt teammates. He had assumed that Malcolm would rejoin them eventually. But Malcolm hadn't returned — for the rest of the hunt, for the rest of last evening, and, it appeared, for all of today until this very moment, which was dusk.

Nina was closing shutters and lighting lamps. She called to Sterling from across the room, "So. Shall I call Detective Divine?"

Sterling groaned and shifted the sofa pillow from under his head to over his face. He said, mostly to himself, "This can't be serious." Nonetheless, a tremor of imminent disintegration came to lodge within his splendidly flat and handsomely tanned stomach. He thought: I can just see the headlines.

Nina, on the way to the phone, also felt a tremor, but of quite a different quality. She was about to dial Tyler Divine's phone number which she, Detective Divine, had given to all parties concerned: "In case there should be developments — don't hesitate to call." As Nina approached the hall mirror she sucked in her own trembling stomach and, squinting into the glass, shifted her aviator glasses from the top of her head to her nose, the better to judge what she saw. Looking hard at herself,

60

she decided: not at all bad. Smiling, she ran a hand through her long dark hair.

What Nina had not told Sterling these last hours, deciding that his travail regarding missing Malcolm needed all their attention, was that at some point during the afternoon's questioning by Detective Tyler Divine, she, Nina, had felt something shift in the region of her heart. It was a feeling that she had all but forgotten was possible. She dialed Tyler's number.

THIRTEEN

Tyler Divine let the phone ring for her service to pick up. In a few minutes she would check to see who had called; it could be an emergency. This was her life now — so extraordinary. In the meantime, she stayed stretched out on the rug in front of the fire and let Joan Sutherland and Marilyn Horne — with the stereo at full pitch — transport her to levels far beyond insistently ringing telephones. As the divas were about to embark on *the* duet, Tyler reached to Alexandra, her Maine coon cat who dozed at her thigh. The cat opened her eyes a tad, and, seeing it was only Tyler, let them close again. The music, the voices, a glass of white wine, a cluster of lit candles of differing heights on a corner table, Alexandra's trusting breathing — dusk.

It had been many months before Tyler could listen to the *Norma;* before she could light candles, before she could sit and remember. The *Norma* had been so much theirs, so much a part of their caring, their love, their lovemaking, their transcendent lovemaking. She mourned less now. The abyss that had been there day after endless day returned only occasionally. The constant knifing ache had abated. She was fairly mended now, not whole, but well enough. She could go on. *Mira o Norma.*

This was Tyler's life now — so extraordinary. Her family refused to comprehend it. But then Tyler always had been out of step. But this? Turning herself into a private investigator? A detective? It was beyond their understanding. And Tyler would not explain.

She reached for her trench coat. "Be good Alexandra," she called out to the cat, who was puffed out at her most voluminous and staring at Tyler from across the room. "Off to work," she continued, to no one. Nina Petrovich's phone message had sounded urgent.

FOURTEEN

"Well, that about wraps it up. Any details you've left out?" Tyler's steady blue eyes bored into Sterling's tired gray ones.

Worn out from having to reveal that which he had selectively kept secret for years, Sterling grew defensive under Tyler's gaze. "Are you insinuating?" he said.

"Just routine," Tyler responded.

Sterling said, "It looks bad, doesn't it?"

"Why do you say that?"

"Well, I was the last to see Malcolm."

"Why do you say that?"

"Well —"

Tyler said, "Many people were out and about — treasure hunting. Anyone could have seen Mr. James after you . . . " She smiled, "left him."

"Then you don't suspect me?" Sterling brightened, pleased to see Tyler's smile.

"I didn't say that. However, suspect you of what?"

"Well, of murdering Malcolm."

"Oh? Has there been a murder?" Tyler smiled again. Her voice was no longer a monotone. In fact, Sterling thought, her last words were a tease. Abashed, he grinned with relief. So the detective was human.

"No body, Mr. White," Tyler continued. "And until, and if, there is one, Malcolm James is simply a missing person, not at all a corpse — although it *is* curious that so many of you think he's been murdered."

Tyler closed her notebook and stood.

Now that she had become real to him Sterling thought: I wonder what her story is?

But Tyler was holding out her hand and saying, "Thank you for coming forward, Mr. White. I appreciate that it undoubtedly was not an easy decision. Will you say goodbye to Ms. — oh."

Nina had materialized, as if she had been listening outside the door, which she hadn't, but she had been waiting nervously within earshot.

"There you are," Tyler said to her.

"Yes," Nina said, breathless, blushing. "Here I am."

The women's eyes met and held.

Sterling looked at them and out of thin, albeit vibrating, air, the thought seized him: This could be a dynamite couple. Breaking the silence that held them he said, exaggeratedly, consulting his watch, "Damn, I'm late," and turned to Tyler to ask if he was free to go.

Tyler, blinking at Nina before turning to Sterling, said, "Of course. You can even leave town. Remember, there is no body."

"Oh, I'm not leaving town," Sterling said, catching Nina's eyes. "Just going over to Jay and Webb's for dinner."

Nina, in a fog, thought: Dinner? What dinner? But before she had time to speak Sterling winked at her, nodding toward Tyler who had turned away to pick up her trench coat.

Oh, Nina mouthed. The flutter in her stomach which had escalated upon her arrival in the living room was now a body-wide tremor. "Oh," she managed to squeak cheerily, "I forgot. In all the commotion, I completely forgot you wouldn't be here for dinner, that you're going to Webb and Jay's and they're such good cooks and Content is off in Philadelphia and I'm alone and the fresh pasta and the pesto and — Detective Divine, would you care to stay for dinner?"

Tyler was startled. Dinner? How long had it been since she had dined with a woman, alone with a woman, or a man for that matter, or anyone . . .

"Good idea," Sterling said as he went to the hall coat tree. "Great idea. Good for you both. It's been a hell of a time." He hurried into his coat and threw one end of his scarf over his left shoulder. "I shan't be late, Nina. No need to wait up."

And he was gone, leaving the two women facing each other. Two women, close in age, close in height, both stunning, one dark, the other with silver blonde hair; one, usually sophisticated, squeaking and trembling, the other only now realizing what seemed to be happening, frowning, attempting to distance herself by shutting off her eyes, her astonishing blue eyes, by stepping backward, only to list off balance, the other reaching out a hand to steady her, saying, her voice not squeaking now, "Do stay," taking Tyler's trench coat, "I'll hang this up."

Later, they were in Nina's upstairs study, Nina showing Tyler some Japanese editions of her mysteries. They were turning the pages of one of the books, like two kids who hadn't yet learned to read, staring at the incomprehensible type, when Nina pointed to a page and said, "Here, right about here, the heroine realizes . . . or, maybe it's here," she was pointing to the facing page, which looked just like the other, "the heroine . . . or, wait, maybe," she turned the page, "it's here." By which point they were laughing helplessly, looking up from the book and at each other. "The heroine," Nina continued — they were still laughing and still looking at each other — "realizes . . . she realizes she's in danger." They stopped laughing. And then they kissed.

And then they talked. And talked, saying things they hadn't said at dinner, things they hadn't talked about with anyone. Tyler spoke of Kim's death, Nina of her troubles with Content. They drank a good deal of brandy. Eventually, exhausted and confessing a mutual need to be held, they moved to Nina's bedroom, where, fully-clothed, they fell asleep in each other's arms.

FIFTEEN

Content Beebe, seeing few lights on in the house, opened the back door carefully and motioned to Bettina to enter quietly. "They've gone to bed early," Content said, referring to Nina and Sterling. "That's luck." She had not wanted to confront Nina about their fight at Hilary's dinner party until morning, and had thought to sneak up the backstairs to the attic-studio. She had brought Bettina along as a buffer, just in case.

In the kitchen she said to Bettina, "I'll put some coffee on. Put your coat in the hall. Here, take mine, okay?"

Bettina walked to the hallway with their coats. Nuts, she thought. When Content had called her from Philadelphia to say she was driving to Cape Gull and had something extremely important to tell her, Bettina had agreed to the meeting only because she had hoped to catch a glimpse of Nina on her home turf. Now, Nina was asleep. Nuts.

She reached the hallway and was lifting her and Content's coats to the hall coat tree when her arm brushed a raccoon fur-lined trench coat. She stared at it, looked away, then did a double take. Her eyes traveled up the hall staircase. Then they swiveled back to the trench coat. Uh oh, she thought. A confused instant of jealousy and excitement ensued. Then she grinned widely, lifted the trench coat from the coat tree, and took it to the hall closet. Before closing the closet door she removed a "Sisters Unite" button from her overalls and attached it to the trench coat's lapel. Then, looking up the staircase once again, and still smiling widely, she sang, rather than said, Oh my oh my oh my.

Back in the kitchen Bettina asked Content what her important news was. She knew she had to keep Content talking. Bettina wondered if she drank. Get her drunk, that's it. And get her up to her attic room. Somehow. Content seemed to be cooperating. She was opening a brandy bottle.

"Want some?" Content asked Bettina.

"Sure," Bettina said, even though like most of her generation she did not drink. I'll sip, she decided.

"Come on," Content said, "let's go into the living room."

"Oh no — no, it's so cozy here in the kitchen."

69

Content shrugged.

"So?" Bettina said. "Tell me your important news."

Content breathed deeply and said, "Last night I saw Malcolm lying in the sand."

Bettina's mouth opened wide, but before she could speak they heard a noise at the kitchen door.

Content jumped up, strode to the door and collided with Sterling. She swiveled to face Bettina, her look saying: Mum's the word.

Bettina, relieved that help had arrived in the person of Sterling, nodded.

"Well," Sterling said. "What're *you* doing here?" He looked at Bettina. "Both of you."

"You're supposed to be asleep," Content retorted.

Bettina caught Sterling's eyes and gestured wildly with her eyebrows. He caught on immediately. "Just having some brandy," Bettina said. "Join us? Please." Her eyebrows went all crazy again.

"Thank you," Sterling said. "Certainly. Hard to pass up brandy on a cold winter night. I'll just put my coat away." This time his eyebrows told Bettina to follow him.

"I'll go with you," Bettina said. Then she lied, "I brought you my book; it's in my backpack."

Once in the front hallway Bettina opened the closet door and pointed to Tyler's trench coat and the "Sisters Unite" button she had pinned to its lapel. Her eyes swiveled up the staircase. Sterling's followed. "Oh my," he said. They nodded at each other.

"All right, then," Sterling said, "we've work to do. Are you with me?"

"All the way," Bettina said.

They returned to the kitchen where Sterling poured himself a brandy and proceeded with all of his considerable expatriate charm to get Content roaring drunk, and, eventually, with Bettina's help, to get her up the stairs to the attic studio where he tucked her into the daybed and locked her in the room. Then he rescued Tyler's trench coat from the downstairs closet and, smiling at the "Sisters Unite" button, took it to Nina's room. He entered quietly, woke only Nina, who almost screamed but for his hand over her mouth. He whispered, "Content's here."

Nina, eyes wide, slipped out of bed and walked with Sterling to the other end of the room. Sterling explained that Content was passed out in the attic and locked in, and together (aided by Sterling's strong encouragement) they decided not to wake Detective Divine, but to set the clock-radio for extra early. Sterling promised to be at hand at five a.m. in case of complications. They hugged goodnight. When Sterling was gone Nina fully took in the astonishing fact that Tyler Divine was asleep in her bed. She decided that there was no way Content would understand. She herself was bewildered. However, she knew, and she knew Content did not, that sex was one thing, loving-sex another, and holding someone through the night — and being held — well, still another. She would deal with Content in the morning. She should have dealt with Content months ago. She slipped back into bed.

Downstairs Sterling put his arm around Bettina, who was putting on her coat. "We did it," he said. "I owe you many thanks." Remembering Bettina's crush on Nina, he added, "It was admirable of you."

"My pleasure," Bettina said, not without a smidgen of wistfulness, but thankful for Sterling's sensitivity. "Do you think Content's really out for the night?"

"Oh my yes. And I'm a light sleeper. And you? Will you get home all right? I really do have to stay and stand guard."

71

"No problem," Bettina said, half-pleased and half-put off by Sterling's pre-liberation courtliness.

"Well then, goodnight and be well. I plan to read your book tomorrow." They shook hands.

Once on the street Bettina slipped the hood of her parka up and slid into a jog, counting gaslights as she bounced along the deserted streets. A new fantasy came to her: Two naked women; the one with silvery blonde hair forcefully grasps, in her teeth, the green eyeshade tangled in the other's long, dark, lush hair, tosses the eyeshade aside — and returns to take the darker woman's freed tresses in her mouth. Yummers.

Six hours later, at five a.m., Sterling was roused from a light sleep by the rattling of the attic door: Content wanting out. Sterling jumped from bed. Naked, he rushed into the hall to the attic door, yelling to Content that the door seemed to be stuck, telling her to hold on, he'd try to fix it. He made some noisy false attempts at opening the door, then told her to keep holding on, he would get some tools.

Content, mightily hung over, sat on an attic step and waited.

Sterling ran to Nina's room at the other end of the hall and found himself interrupting a farewell embrace. The women, although momentarily startled by Sterling's gesturing presence, immediately rallied. Tyler, hustling into her trench coat, hurriedly went around the room in search of her scarf. Nina scurried about helping, as did Sterling, all three beginning to pant with anxiety and bumping into each other. From down the hall came noises of Content trying to open the attic door again, yelling for Sterling.

Tyler, having found her scarf, and ready to leave, embraced Nina, and as they parted Nina pointed to the "Sisters Unite" button on Tyler's trench coat. Tyler grinned. Then all three of them, pretty much out of breath, came together for a three-way hug — and Tyler was gone, leaving Nina and Sterling in freeze positions staring after her.

It was only then that Sterling and Nina came to consciousness about the fact that Sterling had no clothes on. He put a hand over his genitals.

Once downstairs Tyler slipped out the front door into what was still night, stopping on the doorstep to put on her boots. Flushed with disbelief, for a moment she did not know which way to turn.

SIXTEEN

Sunday

"Dru, wake up, Dru." It was Hilary, fluttering, shaking her from sleep. "Farnsworth has disappeared."

Dru let Hilary's words seep into her jumbled psyche and, pulling a pillow to cover her head, mumbled, "Farnsworth is always disappearing."

"This is different," Hilary said, promptly removing the pillow from Dru's face. The pillowcase was edged with elaborate heavy lace which always scratched Dru, but Hilary reminded that it was period. The lace. Befitting the Poplar House. What is the sense of having an authentic Victorian bedroom and Vera linens. Dru, who had grown up with her peripatetic divorced mother in various luxury hotels, couldn't have cared less. She left household details to Hilary, who was now pulling off covers and saying, "Sarah is upset that Farnsworth never showed up for Detective Divine's questioning yesterday. Get up, come on. It's going to be a fraughtful day."

Fraughtful? Dru thought, stretching to ease sleep kinks.

"Maggie is thinking of going home to Philadelphia," Hilary continued. "And I'm wondering if I should go with her. Perhaps I should."

"Why?" Dru asked, distracted, still stretching.

"Why?" Hilary repeated. "Why, to be with her. What if she walks into their apartment and finds Malcolm murdered on their living room carpet? I would be there to hold her elbow to steady her. Well, what do you think? Should I go?"

"What do I think?" Dru said, fully awake now. "I think it's strange how everyone assumes Malcolm has been murdered. With nothing, absolutely nothing, to go on. Except our collective dislike of him. Just like a Perry Mason mystery — everyone having despised the deceased when he was alive, had a terrific motive for wanting him dead." She laughed and put her arms around Hilary. She whispered in her ear, "Good morning." It was a sexy greeting, throwing Hilary off course and making her wonder what had come over Dru lately with all her wet kisses and things. "Well, good morning to you too, darling," she said. "Now get up. I can't begin to imagine what today will bring."

"For one thing," Dru suggested, "probably the beautiful Tyler Divine asking about *two* missings, or is it *three,* counting old Content. Is she coming back to be questioned?"

"No word from Nina," Hilary said. "I'm waiting to phone her. She is such a late sleeper. Now *this* is the last time, darling — Get up!"

Later, when Hilary telephoned Nina, saying she hoped she hadn't called too early, Nina did not say that she had been up for hours, sitting in the kitchen and drinking cup after cup of coffee, talking first with Sterling (while Content took one of her endless baths), trying to piece together how the extraordinary event of Tyler Divine having stayed the night had happened, then with Sterling and Content together, and then with Content alone, finally letting months and months of bottled up frustrations fly, determined not to slip back into the quicksand yet again. Not this time. But not wanting, either, to leave Content there in the muck, but to pull her out, to try, one last time, to get Content to want to step onto firm land.

Content, however, heard what she wanted to hear. Just another set-to, she decided, pleased, for she thrived on them. She was a quicksand lover. She knew no other way to be. And Nina had participated for two years. Secure in that fact, Content reached for another slice of cinnamon toast.

SEVENTEEN

Sunday, 10 a.m.

Oh my lovelies!

The plot, as they say, thickens. Guess who I found in bed with whom? Well, I didn't actually see them, Sterling White did, but I knew they were there. Who with whom? Green eyeshade with the beauteous Tyler Divine. You know, she of the shamus persuasion. You'll be proud to hear that I swallowed my jealousy in best non-monogamy political correctness. Truth to tell, I found the thought of them together sexy; got turned on; have a new fantasy . . .

As to other things, still no solution to the supposed murder. Hilary is all aflutter, left-braining her way through the whole mess. Everyone is on edge. You see, many of everyone's alibis would reveal that they're queer. BIG DILEMMA. It's hardly a prideful "out of the closets and into the streets!" Rather, out of the closets to avoid a prison cell. It's not the best way toward heightened consciousness, but it certainly is one way.

As for details, odd Farnsworth has disappeared. And Maggie, wife of missing Malcolm, hasn't stopped drinking since yesterday morning when Divine came to grill us. Webb and Jay seem little concerned (they're the most out), and Samantha Cake seems too busy turning himself into a herself to get involved in something as distracting as a murder. Content — goddess, what a pill; we (Sterling White and I) locked her in the attic so that Nina and the dyke-dick (sorry, irresistible) could, as they say, MAKE LOVE — I assume. I will always love Sterling for this. Even if he turns out to be the murderer.

I've not had so much fun since I set up the People *magazine reporter, he of the penny loafers, who tried so very hard to be so very hip about homosheckshooality. We have so few perks in our line of work — those of us at the barricades — that playing with sincere journalists — especially* Time *Inc.-ers — fills us, I should say me, with enough glee to keep going.*

Today I have a lunch date with Sarah Lightfoot. I think she has a crush on me. I like her too. Then we're going to see the wetlands. Wetlands? you city women may well ask. Swamps, if the truth be known. Ecologically fragile and extremely important to birds of many hues and

many venues. A far cry from our Manhattan cement. I'm thinking of getting one of those tweed hats English women who stride a lot wear. Sarah has one. She looks cute in it.
   Not a whiff of the media. Thank the goddess.
   More anon.
   Many, many hugs and many, many kisses.

Yours,

Bettina

EIGHTEEN

Bettina was just about to get out of bed and face the day, having finished a letter to her sister communards, when her bedroom door opened to reveal Maggie, wearing a flannel floor-length nightgown and clutching to her breast a bottle of champagne, a carton of orange juice, and two glasses. "May I come in?" she said. "I have to talk."

As she neared the bed, Bettina speculated that Maggie already had had a few. When she climbed under the covers next to her, without so much as a by-your-leave, Bettina was certain that Maggie had had more than a few.

"Mimosas," Maggie said. "I brought two glasses." Bettina decided to have just one. Champagne for breakfast, she mused. How very Cary Grant. She thought of the polka-dotted silk foulard she had slipped into her pocket one rainy afternoon in Bloomingdale's Men's Shop. Alas, she had left it in New York.

"It smells funny in here," Maggie said.

"Pot," Bettina said. "I smoke right before going to sleep. It makes slithering off into the night full of pleasure. And then a few tokes in the morning set up the day."

"Marijuana?" Maggie said, grinning conspiratorially. "I never did it."

Bettina, ever ready to light another joint and share it, caught herself. She thought of what her three-hour feminist talk Friday might have done to Maggie-Doris Day, and decided to nix the dope.

Maggie poured the drinks. She touched her plastic glass to Bettina's — a silent movie clink — and said, "I did not kill Malcolm. I wanted you to know that."

Truth? Bettina wondered.

Maggie drank, mixed another, leaned to kiss the younger woman's cheek and said, "However, I just love that he's dead."

Dru, on her way to her sister's bedroom, encountered Maggie in the upstairs hallway and was about to make morning conversation, but Maggie just smiled oddly, blew her a kiss, and sped down the hall.

81

"Was Maggie just here?" Dru asked Bettina on entering her room after knocking.

"Hi. Yup."

"I would have sworn she was tipsy."

"Drunk."

"Really? Oh, well, I guess we can't blame her." Dru settled herself on the bed. She was wearing red flannel pajamas, a Christmas gift from Hilary. Bettina was wearing a sweat shirt on which was printed: "SO MANY WOMEN, SO LITTLE TIME." Dru chuckled. She leaned to kiss Bettina's cheek. "So, my darling baby sister, how are you this morning?"

"Well-kissed," Bettina answered. "First Maggie, now you. Feels like home. But to answer your question — I'm not sure how I feel."

"*Not* like Friday night," Dru said.

"Not like what?" Bettina asked.

This was the first chance the sisters had had to talk privately since Friday's party. Most of yesterday had been spent catering to Maggie and the disappearance of Malcolm. And then there was the phone call from Content, her asking to see Bettina. By the time Bettina got home, the others, exhausted from the day, had gone to bed.

Dru was continuing, "Flirting with Nina that way at the party. You were quite outrageous."

"Oh. You noticed?"

"Noticed! Didn't everyone? Following her to the john — then during the treasure hunt helping her on the jetty rocks and all."

"She was wearing those high-heeled boots."

"Nina is an expert athlete. Runs the mile in — in no time at all; does yoga, and plays tennis with Sarah Lightfoot practically every day."

Bettina groaned. "Unlike the Marx sisters."

Dru smiled. "Unlike us. But even before that, at the party, when Hilary announced the treasure hunt teams and you and I and Nina and Maggie were put together — well, you feathered out like a peacock."

"Peacocks are male. And you forget Sarah Lightfoot. Sarah was very disappointed not to be on my team."

Dru raised one eyebrow. "And what does that mean?"

"Oh, nothing."

Dru looked deep into her sister's eyes and said, "Nina Petrovich is old enough to be your mother."

"As are you, you know."

"Well, yes, but . . . "

"But what?" Bettina teased. "Anyway, Nina would have had me at age seventeen, hardly likely for someone heading for Vassar."

"All right, all right," Dru said. "Truth? I'm finding it hard to deal with you as a sexual being. I used to change your diapers, for god's sake. And here you are coming on to my friends."

"Best talk to Mother about the diapers. It was her weird doing — sleeping with Dad that way after they'd been divorced all those years. And if we really want the truth, neither you nor Mother ever changed a diaper in your lives. As for Nina, don't worry, it's nothing."

"Nothing? So soon?" Dru was relieved.

Bettina thought of last night at Nina's house, of hiding Detective Divine's trench coat in Nina's closet and then helping Sterling to get Content good and drunk and asleep. She was about to drift off into her new fantasy: Two naked women in a meadow of flaming poppies, the one with silvery . . . but her sister was saying, "On the subject of Mother — here." She reached into her pajama

83

pocket and handed Bettina an air letter. "Yesterday's mail."

"Neat stamps. Russia?"

"Bulgaria. She's fallen in love again. Says he's awfully handsome, in a Bulgarian sort of way. He's thirty."

"Thirty! Mother could be —" Bettina grinned. So did Dru. "His mother!" they shouted simultaneously. They linked little fingers.

"What goes up?"

"Smoke."

"Down?"

"Ms. Claus."

"Close your eyes. Make a wish."

Silence.

"Ready?"

"Ready."

"You know what we should do," Bettina said. "We should fly over for a visit. I haven't seen old Mom in three years. I'll bet she doesn't even know I've become a person of the lesbian persuasion."

"Oh yes she does." When Bettina looked incredulous, Dru said, "The International *Herald Trib*."

"In Bulgaria?"

"Here." Dru handed her the letter. "Read it later."

Bettina put the letter on the bedside table and said fondly, "Goddess, old Mom is weird."

Dru, who had been investigating a pillow, agreed. "Why is this pillow wet?" she asked.

"Maggie," Bettina said, distracted, picturing her mother at a sidewalk cafe table in Plovdiv.

"Crying?" Dru asked, her voice soft.

"Champagne."

"Oh." Dru tossed the pillow aside. "So tell me, what did Maggie have to say?"

" 'I did not,' and I quote, 'kill Malcolm.' "

"Well, that's a relief."

" 'However, I just love that he's dead.' "

"What?"

"You heard right."

"For goodness sake." Dru paused, frowned, decided to continue. "Something's been bothering me about Friday night. Remember how Maggie disappeared when we were walking home from the treasure hunt? You were up ahead helping Nina the athlete walk. And remember how Maggie didn't rejoin us until we reached the house?"

Bettina was staring at her sister.

Dru stopped talking and made a face. "For god's sake, listen to me. Damn Malcolm for doing this to all of us. How could Hilary have such a brother?"

Bettina laughed. "Mr. James, senior, did It with Mrs. James. Simple: Malcolm."

Dru, buoyed by Bettina's joke, said, "I am certain that Mr. and Mrs. James, senior, never did It."

"That's what all of us say about our parents."

"Except the Marx sisters," Dru said, patting their mother's letter. "So. Now that family matters are dispensed with, what I really want to know is what Content had to say last night. What was so urgent? And, by the way, Farnsworth has disappeared."

"I know about Farnsworth. I ran into Hilary near the bathroom on her way to wake you. As for Content — goddess, what a pill. Do you like her?"

"She's the choice of our dear friend Nina."

"What kind of answer is that?"

"Content has her moments," Dru said. "Why did you agree to meet her if you can't stand her?"

Bettina grinned. "She said we'd meet at Nina's house. She wanted me as a buffer because of their fight at the party."

"Aha. But I thought you said, and I quote, 'And as for Nina, don't worry, it's nothing.' "

"Well, it wasn't then, nothing, earlier, but not later, after we got to Nina's house . . . but it *is* nothing."

"What're you talking about?"

"Nothing."

Dru frowned. "So what did Content have to say that was so urgent?"

"She said she had seen Malcolm lying in the sand."

"Lying in the sand!"

"And then Sterling came home and she clammed up. You know how paranoid she is. I'm assuming she'll tell Detective Divine. Why she called me in the first place I'll never know. She thinks I like her. I don't. Talk about fantasy. As was said of Margaret Anderson, Content Beebe's greatest enemy seems to be reality."

Dru beamed. "That's wonderful. You always were a smart kid. What did Nina say?"

"Nothing. When we got there Nina was . . . asleep."

"Lying in the sand?" Dru mused. "How very odd. When? Where? Content had *better* tell Detective Divine. When Hilary talked to Nina a little while ago she said Nina sounded preoccupied. Maybe it was because Content had told her."

Bettina mumbled, "*Very* preoccupied, I'm sure."

"What did you say?"

"Nothing."

Dru got up from the bed. "You certainly say nothing a lot."

Bettina grinned and asked, "What do you make of Detective Divine?" She had decided to tell no one of Tyler Divine's presence in Nina Petrovich's house last night. She felt protective of the women.

Dru returned to sit on the bed. "Well, besides being one great beauty, I was impressed with her competence. Very professional." Dru, who had never held a job, was in awe of women who did.

"Do you think she's lesbian?" Bettina asked, curious to see her sister's reaction.

Dru shook her head and made another face. "Next you'll be saying that . . . that . . . Sarah Lightfoot is lesbian . . . or Maggie is . . . or Mother!"

"And?"

"You're impossible," Dru said, fondly, getting up from the bed again.

Bettina joined her. "Give us a hug," Bettina said, opening her arms. During the hug Dru said, "Listen, let's have lunch, just the two of us — out. It'll give you a chance to continue to raise my sorely neglected consciousness."

"Can't. I'm having lunch with Sarah Lightfoot."

Dru raised one eyebrow.

"It's nothing," Bettina said, and they both burst into laughter.

"Dinner then?" Dru asked. "Hilary has a gaslight meeting."

"You're on," Bettina said.

"Eight o'clock?"

"Eight o'clock."

When Dru reached the door, Bettina called out, "Hey, Sis." Dru turned. "I'm glad we're finally getting to know each other. And — I've decided I like Hilary a whole lot."

Dru smiled. "Good," she said, "so do I."

"Weird as she is," Bettina added.

"Not as weird as Mother, however," Dru parried.

"That," Bettina said, "is one tough contest."

NINETEEN

Tyler's cat Alexandra stared at her from the bedroom doorway.

"Well, hello," Tyler said, putting aside a yellow legal pad and patting the bed quilt. "Come on, aren't you going to say good morning?" The cat entered the room carefully, walking around its edges and heading toward the cushioned window seat, pointedly avoiding the bed, where, judging from cat hairs, she had spent at least some of the night.

"So *that's* how it's going to be?" Tyler said, getting up and walking to the window seat, smoothing a bright blue velour jumpsuit the color of her eyes. Her hair was uncombed, tumbling everywhere. She sat down next to Alexandra, reached to her and said, "Truce?" Alexandra did not respond. Tyler continued, "What about all the times *you* stay out all night? Doing lord knows what? And then parading around here importantly the next day?" Alexandra stayed still as only cats can. "Right," Tyler said, pulling one of Alexandra's ears, "we'll talk later." She got up and then bent down to look directly into the cat's eyes. She said, "She's a lovely woman, old friend, very lovely."

Tyler returned to the bed, and to the legal pad on which she had written down the left hand side of the page:

Motive
Means
Opportunity

And, on the right, the names of those who had attended Hilary's dinner party. Next to Nina Petrovich's name she had doodled many stars. Okay, she thought, embarrassed by the stars, and running a hand through her hair — Motive.

But she couldn't concentrate. She looked across the room to Alexandra and said, "You're thinking it was odd I didn't come home last night, right? Well, it was odd. You're thinking it wasn't very professional of me, right? Well, it wasn't." She picked up the legal pad again and found herself retracing the stars next to Nina's name. My lord, just like high school. She put the pad aside and reached to her bedside table for her journal.

Sunday morning, she wrote. Alexandra had left the window seat and was poised to leap onto the bed. Tyler

caught her and nuzzled into her neck, whispering into her
ear as she wrote in her journal, *Her name is Nina
Petrovich.* "And, if you must know, if it will reassure,"
she said to the cat, not the journal, "it wasn't about sex."
As if she approved, Alexandra positioned herself snugly
under one of Tyler's arms. Tyler returned to her journal
and wrote: *It's not uncomplicated; she's married. . . .*

Tyler answered the phone.
"Good morning, it's Nina. How are you?"
"I'm well."
"Really?"
"Really."
"Terrific. I was concerned."
"Thanks."
"You're welcome."
They laughed.
"Tyler, about last night . . . "
"Yes, about last night. I want to thank you."
"Really?"
"Really."
"Terrific."
They laughed again. Then they didn't know what to
say. Tyler spoke first.
"I've been trying to work, trying to sort out
yesterday's interviews. I have to check in with Hilary."
"Hilary just called me," Nina said. "Malcolm hasn't
materialized. Maggie is thinking of going home to
Philadelphia." She paused. "Tyler, I've been
thinking . . . "
"So have I. But I have to talk to Content first."
"*Content?*"
"About Malcolm James."

"Oh. Of course. I have work to do too. I left a poor Manhattan clerk-typist gasping her last. I still can't believe you're a detective."

"I find it hard to believe myself, sometimes."

"You even have a trench coat."

"But of course." Tyler thought: How long had it been since she joked like this? "Nina," she said, "I really do want to thank you."

"The pleasure, Detective Divine, was all mine. I'd like to see you. Do you think we should meet?"

"I'd like that — but ... "

"We could have lunch — it would be broad daylight."

"No brandy?"

"And no Keystone Kops morning."

They laughed and said they would talk later in the day. "And Nina," Tyler said.

"Yes?"

"I still can't believe you write mysteries."

After hanging up, Tyler stayed quiet for a while. Then she reached for the legal pad and tore off the page, crumpling it into a tight ball. Stars will have to wait, she said to herself. The problem of what had happened to Malcolm James needed her full attention. She got up and headed down the stairs to her study.

Seated at her desk, after a stop in the kitchen for an apple and a hunk of cheese, Tyler began to map out several scenarios that fell under two headings:

(1) Foul Play
(2) No Foul Play

She tackled the latter, and more probable, first.

No Foul Play

(a) Malcolm James, angry at Maggie James for some reason, is playing a gross joke, and is holed up in a local motel, and will appear sometime today. Or, he has returned home to Philadelphia (by bus? hitchhiked?), and will greet his wife when she returns to town.

(b) Malcolm, symbolically going out for a pack of cigarettes, as legions of husbands (and some wives) before him, motivated by something only he could make clear, has disappeared to another town, another life, another identity. Thus, an official Missing Person.

(c) Malcolm, having sobered up after his encounter with Sterling White in the dunes, had been too embarrassed (shocked?) to return to the party. Question: Was Malcolm's time with Sterling a first? Or is he routinely bisexual? Note: Talk to the other members of his treasure hunt team — Content, and Farnsworth when he returns. And talk to Maggie again, alone, out of reach of Hilary's hovering. The question of Malcolm's possible bisexuality could be important. Ascertain.

(d) Malcolm, overcome by his encounter with Sterling, if it was a first, walked into the sea. Unlikely.

(e) Malcolm, still drunk after his time with Sterling, accidentally stumbled into the sea and drowned. Unlikely.

(f) Amnesia after an accidental fall (a blow on the head?) seems improbable. The town's too small. Driver's license, credit cards . . .

Tyler paused and reread what she had written. Right, she said to herself. Now:

Foul Play

(a) Malcolm was killed by someone in an act of random violence, his body dumped. Farfetched, in a town like Cape Gull. This is not New York City.

(b) Malcolm was murdered by someone in an act of revenge. A disgruntled client? Was/is he a criminal lawyer? Ascertain.

(c) Malcolm was murdered by someone who had attended Hilary's dinner party, his body disposed of. Therefore:

Motive
Means
Opportunity.

But first — talk to Content and to Farnsworth.

However, when Tyler called Nina's house to ask for Content, Nina said Content had gone for a walk, and, since Content did everything in double slow motion, lord knew when she'd return. Once, Nina sighed, Content had been two days late for a dinner date. And Sarah Lightfoot, when Tyler reached her, told her that her brother had not been in touch. But, she added, he was never gone for more than a day and a night. She promised to have Farnsworth call Tyler as soon as he returned.

Tyler called Nina again.

"Another business call," she said, when Nina answered. "One question: Is Malcolm bisexual?"

"Malcolm? Good god, no. He's the world's biggest hater of homosexuals."

"Exactly," Tyler said.

"What does that mean?"

"I'm not sure. But I've been reading a book about a phenomenon the author calls homophobia. Irrational fear of homosexuality — which the author, a psychiatrist, posits as a mental illness. He also speculates that the illness sometimes houses itself in certain homosexuals, those who spend great amounts of energy denying they're gay by attacking everyone who is — to protect themselves, of course. Too threatening."

"Interesting!" Nina said. "As we know, Malcolm did make it with Sterling. But I think of that as a fluke, a drunken fluke."

"Let's think again. You've known him a long time. Any thoughts?"

Nina reflected. She had known Malcolm for years. "As I told you last night, we did have that one date — eons ago. Hilary introduced us. He made no overtures. But that proves nothing. Dating in our day seldom included overtures. As I remember, we held hands in the movies. My arm fell asleep. Who knows what he was feeling." Nina laughed. "Maybe that episode proves I was lesbian even then. In my Peter Pan collar and circle pin, good little Vassar freshman that I was, on a working scholarship. Washing all those mountains of dishes. While Hilary, a senior, was fooling around with Miss Meaker, our golf instructor — but I told you all this."

"I want to hear more about you and Vassar and Hilary and Miss Meaker, but at the moment," Tyler said, "it's Malcolm James who's on my mind."

"I shudder for you. But I don't know how I can help ... unless. Maybe I could ask Sterling. You know — how it was, what Malcolm said or did during their ... exchange."

"Is Sterling there? I'll ask him."

"He's in the sun room. I'll get him."

*****

"Good morning, Detective Divine."

"Hello, Mr. White."

"Sterling, please. What can I do for you?"

"Something we didn't go into during our last talk, if you don't mind. It's really only one question. It would help my investigation to know if Malcolm James is routinely bisexual."

"Heavens. How would I know? I only met the man night before last."

"What I mean is, did he say anything or do anything to lead you to believe . . . "

"Well, to spare you the graphic details — we *said* nothing."

"Would you mind describing again exactly what happened?"

"Not in the least. I had left Farnsworth on the path on our way to the old fort — actually, everyone calls it the fort, but it's really an old shore gun battery, a pile of concrete ruins left over from World War Two surveillance of those German U-boats that popped up now and again in the Atlantic. At any rate, I left Farnsworth on the path and went off to — well, to pee . . . "

"Excuse me," Tyler said. "You said you left Farnsworth on the path. Did you mean Farnsworth and Content?"

"No, no — actually, Content had gone off earlier, down to the beach to the shoreline to collect rocks — as she does. We weren't much of a team. Farnsworth hardly said two words to me and jumped whenever I spoke to him. And Malcolm kept wandering off declaring treasure hunts ridiculous and waving his bottle of beer — then meeting up with us later. This was one of the times he wandered off. Content was down by the shore. At any rate, I left Farnsworth on the path. When I got to a sheltered spot in the dunes, about to unzip, there was Malcolm sitting in the sand. He reached out a hand to be helped up — he was quite drunk — and when he stood, well — he groped me. And then, well, one thing led to another."

Nothing like repeating a story, Tyler thought. In their initial talk Sterling had given no details, he simply had said that he and Malcolm had made it. Segued into the dunes, he had put it. Author's license, undoubtedly. No mention of who had made the first move. She asked, "Did he say anything at all?"

"Not a word. But that's not unusual in such encounters. And your next question, to save you embarrassment — Did he know what he was doing? Answer: Yes, he did."

"So," Tyler said, a note of decisiveness in her voice.

"Hold on," Sterling said. "That proves nothing. A million years ago when I nervously made a move for the first time, the gentleman in question did not take me to be a novice, he told me afterward. It does come naturally, you know."

Yes, Tyler thought, it had for her too. She said, "Quite right. But for a moment, let's veer from the sphere of facts. In your *opinion*, would you say Malcolm James was a novice?"

"No," Sterling answered immediately. "And since you're asking for speculation — in my multifarious peregrinations through any number of such occasions I've met many Malcolm Jameses, homosexual men filled with self-hate, men who lead ostensibly straight lives, venturing into their true feelings only anonymously in various darkened corners of this earth . . . my, rather

97

eloquently said, if I do say so. But remember, this is only speculation. And incidentally, there's no doubt in my mind that the self-hate is societally induced."

Tyler asked if Sterling had heard of the book about homophobia she was reading.

Sterling had, indeed. "My editor sent me the bound galleys — not for a quote, mind you, he knows I'm closeted — so is he — but he thought it would interest me. And it certainly did. The gentleman, or lady, protesteth too much, you know. Of course, the present conservative administration in Washington is full of these types — deeply closeted right wing homosexual men. I get ill simply thinking of them, ranting against gay rights as they do. If one is a public figure, being closeted and silent is one thing. Nothing to be proud of, mind you, but that's another story. However, if one is a public figure *and* an outspoken denigrator of one's essence — well! It's pathetic and it's shameful."

Tyler knew that several of Sterling's most famous books were novelized versions of scandalous political goings-on in Washington. She was certain he knew whereof he spoke. Her thoughts went to her own years of silence at editorial meetings, when she was a reporter, when certain colleagues — all men — made awful jokes, knowing full well that they should be covering the nascent gay rights movement, as they covered other social issues, but instead turning the whole thing into a bad joke, thus dismissing it. She had said nothing at those meetings. She had told herself then it was justifiable, considering not only her precarious token status as one of only two women reporters in the magazine's national news department, but also taking into consideration Kim's celebrity status. However, in truth, she now knew that her silence had been deplorable.

She told Sterling what she had been thinking. Then she said, "Have you ever thought of speaking out?"

"Heavens no," Sterling said. "I leave that to others — and wish them godspeed. There's no doubt that I am burdened with unconscious internalized homophobia myself — as I said, societally induced. How live through the fifties in this country, as I did, without it creeping in? For the moment, I leave such things to others. I recently heard, by the way, that Mr. Isherwood is considering taking such a step. I wish him well. And closer to home, here's our own Ms. Bettina K. Marx. Have you read Bettina's book?"

"Not yet."

"I'm halfway through. It's quite wonderful. Outrageous, but exactly on target. Actually, I was just reading it in the sun room, smiling and laughing out loud. Her irony is magnificent. Perhaps you'd like to borrow it when this Malcolm James business is over."

Tyler said she would, and she thanked Sterling for his help.

"Sorry I couldn't be more helpful," he said. "However, I did enjoy our conversation about the closet. We all should be talking of these things more. My life on Ibiza is so insular, in its way."

"I would also like to thank you for your help this morning," Tyler said, "in a rather awkward situation."

"No thanks needed. I was delighted to be of service. Nina is very dear to me."

"Yes, so I've gathered. Well, thank you again."

"You're entirely welcome. Do you want to speak with Nina again?"

"No, not now. I'll call her later."

"Goodbye, then," Sterling said. "And good luck!"

*****

Tyler returned to her legal pad. Assumptions, she thought, nothing but assumptions. No body. And she had pretty much decided there wouldn't be one. Opportunity, she thought. Well, so far definitely Sterling. She dismissed the idea. He had no motive. At least it appeared so. Blackmail? she speculated. Always a possibility with the closeted famous. Absurd, she decided. But Malcolm James *was* a clever attorney. Whoa, she said to herself, slow down — give Malcolm James some time to reappear. She really had to talk to Content and to Farnsworth. Where exactly had they been when Sterling and Malcolm were in the dunes? Had Farnsworth stayed on the path? Had Content been still down by the shoreline? And after Sterling had left Malcolm — had they seen Malcolm? Stop, she told herself, leave it for now. But she found she couldn't. Her thoughts were racing. She began to list the names of Hilary's dinner party guests.

TWENTY

"But you don't understand. I saw him, dead."
Farnsworth Lightfoot was sweating profusely. Samantha
Cake suggested he take off his jacket — a heavy tweed —
and tell her the story again in more detail. Farnsworth
said he would keep his jacket on, but thank you for
asking. He then repeated the story.

"I was on the path near the old fort, waiting for
Sterling White. He had gone off to — well, to relieve
himself. When he didn't come back right away I decided to

go on to the fort alone. I thought perhaps Sterling had gone there after . . . well, you know. It was difficult to read Hilary's handwriting by moonlight, even though there was a full moon, but I had my pencil flashlight with me. When I got to the fort I didn't find Sterling so I decided to go back up to the path to wait for him, and as I was climbing a nearby dune — there was Malcolm, dead in the sand."

"Lying in the sand," Samantha corrected. "Dead is speculation."

Farnsworth frowned. "At the time, I did think he was passed out drunk. But now!"

"I repeat," Samantha said, "he was not necessarily dead at the time you saw him."

Farnsworth blinked, hoping, but not feeling, that Samantha was right.

Smiling, Samantha stood to her considerable height. "Here," she said, "let me refresh your coffee."

She wore a brightly colored flowered silk robe that made swishing noises as she moved. My, she is tall, Farnsworth observed.

From the kitchenette, which was in an alcove off the living room of her one-bedroom apartment, Samantha said to Farnsworth, "Continue, won't you? It helps to talk."

Instantly shy at the word help, Farnsworth looked into his lap. He was still flustered at finding himself in Samantha Cake's Philadelphia apartment this early Sunday morning — after having stayed the night on her sofa! And he was very off balance talking to her so openly. But all of yesterday was off balance, he realized. And she *was* a lovely woman. So genteel.

Samantha handed Farnsworth the coffee and sat next to him on the sofa. The silk of her robe settled deliciously.

"And then?" she said, crossing one leg over the other. "When you saw Malcolm lying in the sand?"

"I didn't linger. I immediately turned away and scurried up a dune to the path. A drunken Malcolm James on a deserted moonlit beach was not something I wanted to encounter. When I reached the path, Sterling had returned."

"And Content was not with him, correct?"

"Yes. She had wandered off earlier in search of quartz. She did appear shortly thereafter, however, holding the next clue, which she had found inside the fort. Content is always very good at Hilary's games. She said she had expected to see us at the fort. It's just like her not to have waited."

"Did she mention having seen Malcolm lying in the sand?"

"No."

"And Sterling?"

"We didn't discuss Malcolm. The several times he had parted from our group we were happy for the brief respites from his negativism. What an awful man." Samantha nodded agreement. Farnsworth continued, "I assumed Malcolm would rejoin us as he had the other times he had wandered away. I was pleased when he didn't return to the party. Maggie, his wife, said not to worry. So we didn't. Then, yesterday morning, Hilary telephoned Sarah to tell her we were to appear at her house at one p.m. for questioning by the detective she had contacted to look into Malcolm's disappearance. Actually, Chief Schmertz had contacted him."

"Her. The detective," Samantha explained, "is a very beautiful woman named Tyler Divine."

Farnsworth blinked. "Really? In Cape Gull?"

"So it appears. She was very thorough in her talk with me. And very sensitive. You really should have met with her."

"Absolutely not. I'm not fond of detectives. As soon as Sarah told me about the questioning I knew I wasn't going to appear."

Farnsworth fleetingly thought of telling Samantha about forty years ago — about the detectives, about the Poplar murders. But it was quite enough that he was talking to her at all. She's such a lovely woman, he thought again. Such a lady. He continued, "When it was time to leave for Hilary's I told Sarah to go on ahead, that I needed to get something from my room and I would rejoin her anon. After I was certain she was nowhere in sight I slipped out the side door, started the car carefully . . . the driveway is on the opposite side of the house. It's startling how loud a car sounds starting up when you're trying to be quiet. I did have a moment's pause when I saw you and Jay and Webb pull up in Webb's van. I waited until you were inside Hilary's house. Then I slipped down the driveway into the street and fled."

"And I found you," Samantha said, "last night, right here on the streets of Philadelphia."

Farnsworth blushed, remembering how he had encountered Samantha late last night as he was emerging from the baths. He had spent the day, as was his periodic wont, first roaming the art galleries, then having a late lunch, then seeing two porno movies, and then spending hours in the baths, mostly watching, but not entirely, finally emerging onto the street energized for another few weeks, heading for the Barclay. The Barclay always had an available room, he being such a regular customer every few weeks, even if sometimes he did have to take a suite.

But last night — there had been Samantha. Farnsworth wasn't clear as to whether Samantha had seen him exit the baths. They encountered one another on the street. Why hello, she had said. In due course she had graciously invited him to her place, which was nearby, for a nightcap. He, vague from his long day, found himself accepting, so unlike him. Soon after reaching her apartment he had fallen asleep on her sofa. How rude, he had been thinking all morning. But that was another worry. Of course Samantha hadn't seen him emerge from the baths, he decided. The door was unmarked. What could a woman like Samantha know about the baths?

But of course Samantha, who had gone out for beer, knew the street and the baths, her old hangout, only too well. She hadn't been near the place in months. Not yet ready to deal with the sexual manifestations of her transformation, she had been celibate for some time. Men had approached her, men who called themselves heterosexual, men who thought she was a transvestite. Close, she had smiled at them, but no cigar, and had left them to make of that what they would. Plenty of time for sex, she had decided. So much to learn. Slowly. In the meantime, here was Farnsworth Lightfoot in her apartment treating her like a lady. Such a gentleman. Farnsworth, who so obviously had been exiting the baths last night. So Farnsworth is gay, she had thought. We *are* everywhere. And here he sat this morning, poor baby, so nervous in jacket and tie, all very formal — despite having passed out last night — and worried sick about maybe having seen a dead man, and having said nothing. Samantha shifted on the sofa and adjusted the silk robe around her thighs, accidentally brushing Farnsworth's tweeded leg.

"Now," she said, smiling warmly over her shoulder, eyes gently cruising, one finger touching Farnsworth's shoulder, "Don't you think you should call your sister?"

Farnsworth recognized Samantha's look — he hadn't been going to the baths and bars without learning something. But no, how can that be, he thought, do women cruise? He had no experience of that. He must have misread her look. Confused, but strangely excited, he said, "I think I *will* take off my jacket now. It's grown quite warm."

Samantha, unable to control her eyes, reached to help him.

TWENTY-ONE

The Pink Tea Cup was jammed.

"I wonder who all these people are?" Sarah Lightfoot said to Bettina as they headed for the restaurant's last empty table. Sarah had been coming to the place for years, ever since Agatha Turnbill, widowed young, had opened the first floor of her house (there were linen table napkins then) to feed the summer people. Nowadays, Mrs. Turnbill's youngest daughter Agatha Junior ran the place with the help of her live-in boyfriend, a young man who liked to cook, and when he did so pushed his shoulder-length blond hair into a ponytail. Agatha Junior had the same blonde ponytail as her young man's, and from the back, in her Levi's, with her slim hips, it was almost impossible to tell whether she was she or she was he. Mrs. T. sat at a table near the exit these days and spent most of her time talking to customers, counting out change slowly and casually from a laminated shoe box that sat on the table, often forgetting a dime, or adding a dime — no one, customers or owner, giving it a second thought.

Just as Sarah and Bettina were settling in at their table, Webb Thatcher and Jay Burloff entered the restaurant; they stopped to greet Mrs. T. "Full up again," Jay said, smiling. "Feels like July. Good for you, Mrs. T. Bad for us."

He spotted Sarah and Bettina. "Happy high noon," he said when he reached their table. He gave each of them a peck on the cheek. Sarah immediately asked him to join them and Bettina concurred. Jay motioned to Webb.

After Agatha Junior left them the chalkboard listing the lunch offerings, Jay looked carefully around the room. "Who are all these people?" he said. "I don't recognize a soul."

"I was just saying the same thing to Bettina," Sarah said.

Bettina, being one of those "from away" as the locals called them, said, "Is this unusual?"

"It is for January," Webb said. "I remember winter weekends when Jay and I were the only customers."

"And don't forget the linen table napkins," Sarah added.

"It's getting so there really is nowhere to go on weekends for a little peace and quiet," Webb complained.

"Spoken like a true businessman," Jay said. Only this morning he had spoken to Webb about perhaps opening their bookshop on Sundays, at least for half a day. "Never," Webb had said. "We didn't leave the city to help build yet another one."

Agatha Junior had arrived to take their orders. She never wrote anything down — merely smiled beatifically — and never mixed anything up. She had been something of a mathematical genius at Cape Gull High School, but on graduation had opted for travel, "at least for a while," before college. When she had returned from Nepal with ponytailed lover in tow, she had asked Agatha Senior if she and boyfriend might manage the restaurant. Mrs. T. had hesitated only briefly, then welcomed them aboard. They had brought with them two young men, Americans from Brooklyn they had met on the beach in Goa. Within months the Pink Tea Cup offered a catering service called the Lavender Express, managed by the two young men who, in Goa, had transformed themselves into personages of the East: Vishnu and Govinder.

After giving Agatha Junior their orders, and after some more bantering about the weekend outlanders, Jay asked, "So, what does everyone make of Malcolm's disappearance? Or has he returned?"

"Nope," Bettina said. "No word at all."

Sarah, who knew about disappearing men, her brother being a prime example, said she thought Malcolm would probably return any time now.

"I wouldn't be too sure," Jay said.

Webb agreed. "Malcolm's the sort of man who likes to drag out things like this just to be annoying. He's certainly done other annoying things in the past. Poor Maggie."

"Like what?" Bettina asked. "What else has he done?"

"Well, once," Webb said, "some summers ago — Sarah knows this story — we had the dubious pleasure of going on a beach picnic with him ... "

Jay interrupted, "Hilary was trying to pawn us off as her and Dru's gentlemen callers." Sarah smiled.

Webb continued, "With our consent, remember. That was before we put a stop to it, before we started the publishing house — before Stonewall."

Jay took up the story. "There we were, picnicking away, when Malcolm yelled out to us — and to everyone else on the beach — that he was drowning. Flailing his arms about, he sank — and didn't surface. Well of course Webb and I, and Dru, jumped into the sea, as did several strangers near us — it was a No Life Guard spot. Anyway, what he had done, of course, was to swim underwater to where the old half-sunken ship sticks up ... " Jay looked at Bettina. "Do you know about the ship?" She said she didn't.

Webb, the student of Cape Gull's history, took over. "It's made of concrete — one of our government's less successful experiments during World War One because of a shortage of steel. When the powers that were finally decreed the idea a bust, the ship was towed here to be used as part of a proposed new wharf. However, one night, under circumstances never clearly documented, the ship broke loose from its moorings and grounded its bulk not far from shore at Flounder Beach — where we were picnicking that day. You can guess the rest. Malcolm swam underwater to the ship and surfaced on the other side of it, out of view of the beach. Later, after Hilary had alerted the Coast Guard, we saw Malcolm sauntering

110

down the beach toward us, yelling, 'What's all the commotion?' "

"Weird," Bettina said.

"A neurotic bid for attention," Jay said. "A short man's specialty." To which Webb immediately said, "Do forgive my friend's unfailing intolerance."

Sarah asked if they had told Detective Divine the story, since it hadn't occurred to her that it might be relevant.

"Sure," Jay said. "And speaking of Detective Divine, what do you make of her? Awfully intelligent, for a gumshoe. She's been in the bookshop several times. Knows her literature. I wondered who she was — somebody's gorgeous house guest was my guess."

"She's really awfully lovely," Sarah said. "She was very kind when Farnsworth didn't appear for the questioning."

"Speaking of disappearing men," Jay said.

"I was hoping you'd ask," Sarah said. "Farnsworth telephoned me this morning. And you'll never guess where he called from."

Agatha Junior arrived with the food. After some pleasant remarks about how big the blueberry muffins were — they were enormous — and after Agatha Junior said, "Enjoy," Jay said, "So, where did Farnsworth call from?"

"You'll never guess."

"Right," Jay said. "So tell us."

"Samantha Cake's."

Jay and Webb stopped buttering their muffins and stared at Sarah. "*What* did you say?" Webb wheezed.

"He was having breakfast with your friend Samantha Cake. In her apartment in Philadelphia."

111

Bettina thought of tall husky Samantha serving bacon and eggs to short round Farnsworth.

"I was quite amazed," Sarah continued. "You know how shy Farnsworth is."

Jay wondered: What the hell was Sam up to? He shuddered to think.

Webb said, "I didn't know they were acquainted."

"They're not, really. I mean they weren't," Sarah said. "They met at Hilary's the other night, and then Farnsworth ran into her this morning in Philadelphia when he was going out for breakfast and she for the Sunday paper. Isn't that a nice coincidence?"

Jay and Webb said nothing. Bettina thought: Weirdness everywhere.

"I always rather suspected Farnsworth's disappearances were only to Philadelphia," Sarah said. She realized, after she had spoken, that she had never discussed her brother's peculiarity quite so casually. My, she thought, pleased, that's two nevers done away with — the first being Farnsworth's telephone call to her this morning to tell her where he was. Perhaps Malcolm's latest shenanigan had its positive side.

Jay was surprised by Sarah's last statement. She seemed full of good cheer, her healthy WASP cheekbones at their shiniest, and he decided that this might be an opportune time to ask about that which was never spoken of, to get Sarah to talk of that about which he had always been curious. He hesitated, knowing Webb would not approve, but buoyed by Sarah's openness and by Bettina's presence — after all, Bettina was someone who did not dissemble, who in her book had told things as they were; someone who paraded around with all those activist buttons and the sky had not fallen — Jay said, "You know, Sarah, I've always been curious. Has Farnsworth ever talked to you about the Poplar murder? What actually happened all those years ago?"

Webb, as Jay had expected, was shocked. "Jay," he said disapprovingly.

But Sarah flinched not at all. "He never has," she said, and added, "Perhaps it's time he did."

Webb, still shocked, apologized for his lover's rudeness.

"Nothing of the sort, Webb," Sarah said. "No need for apologies. We all should talk to one another more." She winked at Bettina, who was gazing at her sister's friends with increasing fondness.

Later, when they were having their second cups of coffee, Jay said to Bettina, "Sterling White bought your book yesterday."

Bettina, accustomed as she was becoming to her recent celebrity status, beamed. It was especially wonderful when another writer read one's book. She was secure enough about the work to have no apprehension about what he would think of it. She was pleased that he had bought his own copy. Webb and Jay had the book displayed in their bookshop's window, along with other books by local authors (mostly Nina's), having decided that books by sisters of locals qualified, but mostly wanting to feature a bold lesbian feminist book for gaping conservative townsfolk. The chapbooks they published were also in the window, but these were quiet books of poetry by gay and lesbian authors who had not been on the Merv Griffin show.

"You know what I've been thinking," Jay said, addressing Bettina. "While you're here — why don't we have a book discussion evening? Maybe we can ferret out some of the closeted types who live here. Who knows who would be courageous enough to come, but certainly our

113

gang. Only gays and lesbians." He looked at Sarah. "Sorry, love," he said to her.

Sarah smiled. "Quite all right," she said, not without a twinge of envy. A book discussion! And featuring Bettina's book! She would dearly love to attend.

"We can throw in some consciousness raising," Webb said.

Bettina was excited. A CR group in Cape Gull. "Fantastic," she said.

"Let's see," Webb said, "who should we invite?"

Sarah, sensing a need for privacy, excused herself and went to chat with Mrs. T.

Jay was saying, "Dru, Hilary, Nina, Content if she's in town, Sterling if he's still here." Then he named others who were not in their immediate circle.

And don't forget Detective Divine, Bettina thought, but did not say.

As Jay spoke, a dazzling winter sun sliced through the lace-curtained window and bounced off Bettina's activist buttons with a glittering energy.

Webb blinked. "There's nothing like January sunlight," he said.

"Right," Bettina said. "Makes you think anything is possible."

TWENTY-TWO

As Tyler approached Nina's house with the prospect of interviewing Content Beebe, she had to admit to a feeling of unease. Although she had never met Content, she had last night's unburdening by Nina as preface. She would have preferred no knowledge of the woman. Objectivity, at least to begin, was essential. Right, she thought, objectivity. Now *there* was a subject. She adjusted the belt on her trench coat and rang the doorbell.

Content, who took her time in answering, had decided she would not tell Detective Divine about having seen Malcolm lying in the dunes near the old fort Friday night. She had assumed he was just passed out drunk, and had left him there. She was now thinking she never should have returned to Cape Gull at all. If she told of having seen Malcolm it would just complicate things; she might have to stick around Cape Gull. She wanted to get home to her cats, and away from Nina's mood. She hadn't even told Nina about having seen Malcolm. She had intended to, but when Nina had started in dissecting their relationship her mind had glazed over and all she wanted was to get away. Of the possible seriousness of the matter at hand Content gave nary a thought. She had successfully wiggled out of any number of serious matters in her time. This would be no different. Besides, Malcolm was just passed out drunk. What was the big deal?

When Content opened the door, she said to Tyler, "Nina and Sterling went out to lunch."

Tyler, momentarily perplexed by the odd greeting, said, "I'm Tyler Divine. You must be Content Beebe."

"That's me," Content said. She was eating a doughnut. "I'd offer you one, but I ate them all."

Standing on the porch with Content not ushering her into the house, Tyler was forced to ask, "May I come in?"

"Sure," Content said. She stepped aside with a theatrical bow.

Once in the hallway Content made no move to take Tyler's coat. Tyler hung it on the hall coat tree. Again Content, concentrating on her doughnut, said nothing, forcing Tyler to say, "Well, where shall we sit?"

"I don't know," Content said. "In the sun room?"

"Fine," Tyler said.

Once they were seated, Content immediately said, "The way I figure it, Malcolm's just foolin' around. I don't know what all the fuss is about."

"Perhaps," Tyler said. "Nevertheless . . . "

"I know. In case he's dead." Content had powdered sugar on her chin, and on her purple sweat shirt. She licked her fingers. "He's not dead. Just foolin' around."

Tyler opened her notebook, and Content said, "What's it like being a detective?" She was looking at Tyler with a sly seductiveness. Somehow, her words had been salacious.

Tyler thought: Screw objectivity. I don't care for this woman at all — Nina's existence aside. She said, "I'd like to ask you a few questions."

"Yes Ma'am!" Content said, saluting.

Tyler, keeping her voice neutral, said, "I'll need your full name and address, and age." Content complied. Tyler wrote in her notebook.

"Next, I'd like to ask you what sort of man Malcolm James is."

"Tough guy. Likes practical jokes."

"Practical jokes?" Tyler said, aware of this fact but wanting to draw Content out.

"Correct. Like once — pretending he'd drowned." She launched into the Flounder Beach story. Tyler listened carefully. It was always of interest to hear the same story told by different people. Jay Burloff had been disgusted in the telling; Content was laughing, telling it as good fun.

When Content finished, Tyler said, "You were on Malcolm James's treasure hunt team, were you not?"

"I were. Me and Farnsworth and Sterling."

"Was Malcolm with you during the entire hunt?"

"Nope. He kept wandering off."

117

"Were the rest of you together at all times?"

"Except for when I found the clue."

"Tell me about that."

"Okay. Sterling and Farnsworth and I were walking toward the old fort — we were up on the path. I told them I would meet them at the fort and then I headed down the dunes to the shore. I was after some Cape Gull gems — there was a full moon and they were glittering away — the wet ones — down by the shore — the ones wet from the waves — they're pieces of quartz — the gems. I've got quite a collection . . . "

"Where did you find the clue?"

"I'm getting to that. I sort of got absorbed in picking up the gems, and before I knew it I was way down the beach, way past the old fort. I sometimes lose track of what I'm supposed to be doing. I had to double back to the fort."

"You found the clue in the fort?"

"Correct. I'm pretty good at clue finding. I expected to find Sterling and Farnsworth there. But they weren't."

"And then?"

"Then I climbed the dunes to the path and met up with them there."

"Malcolm was not with them?"

"Nope."

"And while you were in the fort, and on the beach, you did not see Sterling or Farnsworth or Malcolm?"

"I told you I met up with Sterling and Farnsworth on the path."

"And Malcolm?"

"I told you, he wasn't on the path."

"On the beach, then?"

Content hesitated before she said, "No."

Tyler, noting the hesitation, pressed, "So you're saying that you did not see Malcolm James on the beach near the old fort?"

"Correct."

Content was pleased with herself. She had seen Malcolm lying in the dunes, not on the beach. Thus, technically, she wasn't lying. She was beginning to enjoy this game.

Tyler asked, "Do you remember what time it was when you were in the fort?"

"Nope."

"Any idea?"

"Nope. I don't wear a watch. To tell the truth, I hardly ever know what time it is."

"Well, then, would you tell me again, in as much detail as you can, your actions after leaving Sterling and Farnsworth on the path?"

"Again? Oh." Content's seductive smile was back. "I get it — you're looking for inconsistencies. Okay. As I said, I told my teammates I was going after some gems, and headed down the dunes for the shoreline. I told them I'd meet them at the fort. I walked along the shore and before I knew it I was way down the beach, way past the fort, and had to double back."

"How would you describe where the fort actually is located?"

"It's up in the dunes. Haven't you been there?"

"Which means you approached the fort from the beach?"

"Correct."

"Did you approach it on its left or on its right side?"

"Sort of in the middle . . . no, let's see, to the left — if you're facing it from the beach, as I was. To its right, if you're looking over it from the path above it."

119

"The path being behind the fort."

"Behind and above. Look . . . " Content pointed to a wicker armchair. "Pretend the chair is the fort. Behind the chair, in front of it, and to either side of it are the dunes. And up behind it, on high ground, is the path. Haven't you been there?"

"So you approached the fort from the beach on its left side. And you went inside the ruins."

"Correct."

"And you did not see Farnsworth or Sterling or Malcolm inside the fort itself."

"Correct."

"You found the clue and then you exited. Which way did you turn?"

Content thought for a moment. "Left. I turned left."

So why hadn't she seen Malcolm? Tyler thought. She said, "And then?"

"And then I climbed the dunes to the path."

"The dune you climbed was to the right of the fort?"

"To its right as seen from the beach, right."

"And you met up with Farnsworth and Sterling on the path."

"You got it."

Tyler was silent and Content was absorbed in the right-left puzzle. This was a most interesting game.

Tyler thought: If Sterling was telling the truth, it appeared that he had left Malcolm in the dunes to the right of the fort — as you face the fort from the beach. And it also appeared that during Sterling's encounter with Malcolm, Content, if she was telling the truth, had been down the beach near the shoreline way past the fort. The question was: Why hadn't Content seen Malcolm after she had doubled back to the fort, entered, it, found the clue, and exited — to her left — which would have put her in the same area where Sterling had left Malcolm? There were only two answers: (1) Malcolm had roused himself and had gone off or (2) Content was lying.

In any case, if they both were telling the truth, it appeared that Sterling had had Opportunity. And if Content was lying, so had she. But motive? Either of them? And Farnsworth? Where was Farnsworth during all this? Waiting patiently on the path?

Content had stopped thinking of the right-left puzzle and was staring at Tyler, the seductive smile back again. "That's a lot of detail about the fort," she said. "You a Virgo?"

Isn't it odd, Tyler thought, how a seductive look can look anything but.

"I think you're doing a lot of figuring for nothing," Content was continuing.

"Perhaps," Tyler said. She busied herself with her notebook.

"So," Content said, "how does someone become a detective?"

The woman was downright cloying, Tyler decided. She had no intention of talking to Content Beebe about her life. In fact, she was beginning to feel that the woman was odd in some way. She closed her notebook and said, "How I became a detective is a long story. And I'm late for an appointment." She looked at her watch.

"So this is it?" Content said.

"For now. I want to thank you for your cooperation."

"Anytime," Content said. "Do you want a beer?"

"No, thank you," Tyler said, thinking: Doughnuts and beer.

"How about a Harvey Wallbanger?"

121

"I beg your pardon?"

Content laughed. "It's a drink."

They walked to the hall where Tyler got her coat. "Nifty trench coat," Content said. The seductive smile was now fixed. Tyler fleetingly wondered if Content had seen her coat on that very coat tree last night. But no, of course not, things would have transpired much differently if she had.

Content said, "So you're really not going to tell me how to become a detective?"

Exasperated, Tyler tried for lightness, "First, you get a trench coat."

"I'm serious," Content said. "I always thought I'd make a good sleuth."

Actually, she probably would, Tyler thought. She had an obnoxious doggedness that in everyday social interaction was annoying, but in detective work was usually an asset. She told Content that perhaps she *would* make a good detective. Then she said she really had to be off. "And thank you again, Ms. Beebe, for your cooperation."

"Sure," Content said. She lifted a hand and was about to punch Tyler on the arm, but Tyler slipped out the door.

Once in her car, Tyler thought: So this is Nina's lover — but stopped herself from going any further.

Content watched Tyler get into her car. As she turned from closing the door, her foot hit something on the hallway carpet, causing it to roll onto the oak flooring where it pinged metallically. She stooped to pick up the object. She read: "Sisters Unite."

"Uh ha," she said, recognizing the button as one that Bettina wore on her overalls. Well, well, she thought, her thought now truly salacious: What was Ms. Divine doing with Ms. Bettina's feminist button? "Ho ho," she said, pocketing her secret and lumbering off in search of a beer.

TWENTY-THREE

When the telephone rang at Hilary and Dru's house, Bettina answered in the kitchen. It was Content.

"Listen," Content said. "About what I told you last night? About seeing Malcolm lying in the sand?"

"Yes?" Bettina said.

"Forget it."

"What?"

"Forget I told you, okay?"

"What does that mean?"

"It means I'm asking you not to tell anyone."

"Why? I already told Dru."

"Damn," Content said. "Dru'll tell Hilary, and then —"

"Well," Bettina said, "so what?"

"I decided not to tell Detective Divine."

"You didn't tell Detective Divine?"

"Or Nina."

"You didn't tell Nina?"

"You heard me. Listen, tell Dru not to tell Hilary, if it's not already too late. And not to tell anyone else either."

"This is crazy," Bettina said.

Content was silent.

"Hello," Bettina said. "Hello, you still there?"

"Are you missing one of your activist buttons?" Content's words had slithered.

"One of my what?" Bettina said.

"Like 'Sisters Unite'?"

Bettina was silent.

"Hello," Content said. "Hello, you there?"

What is going on? Bettina wondered. She again said, deliberately not mentioning the button, "This is crazy."

"So are you going to talk to Dru?" Content said.

Had Content found out about Nina and Tyler? Bettina thought quickly. But why is she trying to blackmail me? This is crazy *and* silly. She said, "Dru'll just get suspicious. Why *didn't* you tell Detective Divine?"

"I didn't feel like it. Malcolm's okay, okay?"

"What if he's not? You're just creating more intrigue."

"Malcolm's okay."

"How do you know?"

125

"He was just passed out drunk. Listen, just talk to Dru."

Bettina took a moment to collect her thoughts before she said, "No. That's conspiracy — whatever you're up to. Why don't you talk to Dru yourself?"

"I'll just do that. Thanks, Sister." Content slammed down the receiver.

A pill, Bettina fumed. I said she was a pill.

Dru entered the kitchen, saying, "Who was that?"

"Oh, just Content," Bettina said.

"What did she want?"

"Nothing."

"There you go again," Dru said. "Did she have her interview with Detective Divine?"

"Yes."

"Good," Dru said. Then Content had told the detective about having seen Malcolm lying in the sand. "Maybe we'll get somewhere now. How was your lunch?"

"Neat," Bettina said, relieved by the change of subject. "We're going to have a CR group."

"You and Sarah?"

"No, dummy. Webb and Jay were there. It's Jay's idea. You're invited."

"Me? What for?"

"We're going to discuss my book."

Dru became interested. "In that case," she said, "count me in. But why did you say CR?"

"Habit, I guess. Certainly no one around here needs her or his consciousness raised."

Dru smiled. "Want some ice cream?"

"No thanks. I'm off to meet Sarah again — we're going for a hike to see the wetlands."

"You're certainly seeing a lot of Sarah," Dru said. "Well, have a good time. And don't forget dinner. I thought we'd go to *La Maison.*"

"Sounds fancy."

"It is, somewhat."

Bettina looked down at her overalls.

Dru smiled. "They're fine. But look at you, worrying about what to wear."

"I guess your life is rubbing off on me a little."

"And yours on mine," Dru said, extending her arms for a goodbye hug.

When Dru was certain her sister had left, she dialed Tyler Divine's number.

"Hello, Detective Divine, it's Dru Marx."

"Oh yes," Tyler said. "Hello."

"I'm glad I caught you. I understand you're coming here this afternoon to talk to Maggie again. The reason I'm calling — I don't know how to put this — but it's been bothering me — it's about Maggie." Dru paused. "Remember when you asked me if our treasure hunt team had been together at all times during the hunt?"

"Yes?"

"Well, I wanted to tell you — not that I suspect Maggie of anything, perish the thought — but these unsaid things so often lead to unnecessary confusion, and I'm sure Maggie has an excellent explanation. But, well, when we were walking back to the party, I was talking to her — Nina and Bettina were off ahead of us — and, well, Maggie disappeared."

"Disappeared?"

"Yes. I was talking away, and then all of a sudden she wasn't there."

127

"How was that?"

"I just don't know. Moments before, we had turned a corner from Main Street onto Elm, heading home — it's fairly dark on Elm at that point — all those ancient tall trees, they blot out the moon. And the gaslights — it's the heart of the historic district — the gaslights don't illuminate very well. When I realized she wasn't with me I called out to her but got no response, so I went back to the corner of Elm and Main, but she wasn't there. So I thought maybe she had somehow gone on ahead. But when I caught up to Nina and Bettina, near the Pennypacker House — you know, it's the one with the best barge-boards — Maggie wasn't with them. They asked me where she was and I just said she'd be along in a minute. And she did catch up to us, but not until we reached home." Dru stopped to catch her breath.

Tyler said, "But you said nothing of this when we talked yesterday."

"I know. And it's been bothering me ever since. I'm sure there's a perfectly good explanation."

"How long was Mrs. James gone?"

"I'm not sure. Not long. Ten minutes, possibly more."

"Did she say where she had been?"

"I didn't ask. We were at the house and about to open the gate, and we all just proceeded to walk in."

Tyler did not press Dru about not having come forward earlier. She had learned in her work that people often left out certain information — even lied — for any number of reasons, some innocent, some not. It was all a matter of checking and re-checking everything from all possible angles. She would talk to Dru again, if need be, after she had talked to Maggie James.

Dru was continuing, "I'm so mad at Malcolm for having caused all this."

128

"Yes," Tyler said. "I appreciate your calling. At the moment, all information whether it turns out to be relevant or not is important."

"I agree," Dru said, grateful for the validation. "It's the unsaid things. I feel so much better having told you. I'm certain there's a perfectly good explanation. By the way, Hilary and I plan to be out when you talk to Maggie."

"Thank you," Tyler said.

When Tyler hung up, the telephone rang again.

"Detective Divine?"

"Yes?"

"It's Farnsworth Lightfoot."

"Oh yes. Mr. Lightfoot. Thank you for calling."

"I've just returned from Philadelphia. There's something I . . . I . . . must tell you. I . . . I . . . saw Malcolm James lying in the dunes near the old fort Friday night. I assumed he was passed out drunk. I didn't linger to check. But now . . . I, I . . . perhaps we should meet."

"Yes, of course," Tyler said. Her appointment with Maggie James was two hours away. She asked Farnsworth if he was free now.

"Yes," Farnsworth said. "Will you come by the house?"

"Certainly. Is fifteen minutes all right?"

"Yes, yes, of course."

Tyler decided that perhaps it was time to alert Chief Schmertz. Although Malcolm James indeed could have been dozing when Farnsworth saw him — a possible state after his encounter with Sterling — apparently Farnsworth had not gone near enough to be certain. This coupled with Content's hesitation when Tyler had asked her if she had seen Malcolm on the beach perhaps were developments serious enough to warrant notifying Chief

129

Schmertz. And then there was the matter of Maggie's ten minute disappearance.

But, as she walked to her door, Tyler thought: There's still no body, there's still no crime — there's only the possibility — and just look at how lives have been disrupted. She pondered, not for the first time, the ramifications of the power she held. It was not unlike when she had been a journalist. As a means to a possible end, innocent people could be hurt while the guilty often slipped through loopholes. But then, sometimes, people's lives needed disruption.

TWENTY-FOUR

When Nina and Sterling returned from lunch, Content, holding her beer and Bettina's "Sisters Unite" button, said to them, "It looks as if our little Bettina K. Marx is having an affair with our lovely Detective Divine." After which things went downhill very quickly indeed, ending with Content out the door, in her car, heading home to Philadelphia.

Nina looked at Sterling and said, simply, "I think that that may be that."

Sterling, unable to nod in sympathy, said, "Hallelujah!"

Nina said, "Come on, let's talk." They walked to the kitchen and settled in with coffee and cigarettes.

Nina said, "I think I'm falling in love with Tyler Divine."

"Terrific," Sterling said. "Just plain terrific."

"But I also thought I was in love with Content — once upon a time."

"We all make mistakes."

"I'm so weary of making mistakes," Nina said. "How *does* one know?"

"One doesn't, really. One takes risks. And keeps checking in."

"Or one never takes risks."

"Unlike us."

"Unlike us."

"Falling in love, as S. Freud once said, or is reported to have said, is a temporary state of insanity. Loving is another matter."

"But I thought I loved Content."

"Nina, darling, it's as clear as can be that Content is unable to accept love. She's like your last love — that woman who used the dictionary words."

"You mean my swain?" Nina said, laughing. "Are you saying there's a pattern to my linkages?"

"Many of us have them. Some of us break them."

"I've known Tyler Divine the equivalent of one day."

They both paused. Then laughed.

Sterling said, "What's important here is facing up to the unhappiness of your relationship with Content. What happens with Tyler is yet to be seen. However, romantic that I am, I predict ... "

"That we will walk off into the sunset?"

"It's been known to happen."

"You know, in the old days I already would have sent flowers."

"You mean you didn't?"

"No. This morning we talked about whether or not Malcolm is bisexual."

"Good. You're operating in reality. Good."

"Does reality mean you never send flowers?"

"Perish the thought."

They smiled and were quiet for a while.

"You know," Nina said, "Content thinks relationships just are. Period."

"Not an uncommon stance," Sterling said.

"How could I have been involved with her so long?"

"A therapist once told me, when I was lamenting just such a situation, that things are never one hundred percent bad. One falls in love with the good and doesn't see the bad — at first. And then, when the first warts appear one hopes the person in question will change. A rather common, but dangerous undertaking. The secret is to accept the warts lovingly — if they aren't beyond the pale."

"What a waste of years," Nina muttered.

"Remember, not one hundred percent bad."

"Small solace," Nina said. She realized she was getting somewhat depressed. And as they continued talking she was thinking, Is it worth the risk? She asked the question of Sterling.

"Well, I'd say yes. But only if you won't blame me if things don't work out."

"Don't be ridiculous," Nina said. "It's not a question of blame. I just don't know if I could take another heartache."

133

"Of course you could," Sterling said. "If it comes to that. Which it might not, you know. It might not at all."

That, Nina thought, was a possibility. As much of a possibility as not. Fifty-fifty? Not the best of odds. But then she always had been a gambler.

And sometimes she had won.

TWENTY-FIVE

Tyler and Farnsworth Lightfoot were in the dunes near the old fort.

"It was here," Farnsworth was saying. "Right about here."

It was all as Content had described.

The fort, surrounded by dunes, overlooked the beach and, beyond, the sea. Above it, on high ground, was the path Tyler and Farnsworth had taken to the area. They had had to leave the path and descend the dunes to reach the fort. Tyler noted that they were standing to the right of the fort as seen from the beach. She suggested they circle the fort. Afterward, they entered the ruins, exited, and took another turn around the area. Then they climbed the dunes back to the path.

"I assumed he was passed out drunk," Farnsworth repeated for the third time. "And I didn't linger to check."

Tyler was quiet as they began the walk back to town. Then she said, "Mr. James very well may have been dozing when you saw him, Mr. Lightfoot, but I'm certain you recognize the possible seriousness of your disclosure. I'll have to tell Mrs. James, and Ms. James — Hilary — about this. And depending on their decision, perhaps Chief Schmertz."

Farnsworth, after a moment's hesitation at the mention of the police, said, "Yes, yes, of course." On his trip home from Philadelphia he had begun to feel a strength and well-being he hadn't felt in years — not since his tennis tournament days. He vaguely wondered where his old tennis racquet was. It undoubtedly would need re-stringing. Or perhaps he would buy a new one. Yes, he decided, he would buy a new tennis racquet.

As they passed a bench that faced out to sea, Tyler said, "I want to thank you for coming forward, Mr. Lightfoot. I do appreciate that it must have been a difficult decision." Farnsworth motioned to the bench and said, "Will you sit a moment, Detective Divine? There's something I'd like to tell you."

Once seated, Farnsworth hesitated. He began to breathe rapidly, but calmed himself by looking out to sea. Then he spoke. "This isn't all that relevant to Malcolm's disappearance, but I'm beginning to realize it is most important to me." He paused. "When I learned from my sister that Malcolm was missing and that Hilary had

called in a detective, I experienced a severe anxiety attack
— much worse than those to which I am accustomed —
and, as you know, I failed to show up for your
questioning. I spent yesterday in Philadelphia, rather in a
fog, and it was only with the urging of Samantha Cake,
whom I encountered in the city, that I decided to come
forward. I feel terribly relieved to have done so. It's odd. I
feel a certain strength. I rather expected to feel the
opposite." Farnsworth paused again. When he continued,
his eyes looked directly into Tyler's.

"Forty years ago, when I was ten years old, I think I
witnessed the beginning of what turned out to be a
murder. Actually two murders — in the Poplar House —
Hilary and Dru's house now. The Poplar Affair? Have you
heard of it?"

Tyler said that she hadn't.

"Detectives came to question me. I told them I hadn't
seen anything. It was mostly the truth. I didn't know
whether I had seen anything or not. The night before, I
was in bed, almost asleep, when the light went on in Mr.
Poplar's bedroom — which was opposite to mine. It was
odd, because it was mid-week and the Poplars were in
residence only on weekends, and then only occasionally. I
was curious. I saw Mr. Poplar, who seemed to be laughing
and clowning around with a woman — who was not Mrs.
Poplar. She was young. I was very interested, but I knew I
should pull down my window shade, and when I went to
do so, a light went on in a downstairs room of their house,
and I saw — I saw someone. It was difficult to see clearly
at that angle, looking down, and for a moment I assumed
it was Mrs. Poplar. Then I looked into the upstairs
window again and saw Mr. Poplar still cavorting with the
young woman. And then I lowered my eyes to the
downstairs window but the light had gone out. By then I

realized that I should not be spying on Mr. Poplar like that, so I pulled down my window shade.

"The next day when Mother told me some detectives wanted to talk to me I really didn't know whether I had seen anything or not. It all seemed rather like a dream. And I was frightened. It wasn't until some years later, when I began to know something about life and people's private behavior, that I began to think that perhaps it was Mrs. Poplar that I had seen in the downstairs window. She had discovered the bodies. Perhaps I had seen her, but I didn't know for certain then. And I don't now."

Farnsworth looked out to sea. Then he said, "When Sarah told me yesterday that a detective wanted to ask me some questions about Malcolm, that long ago memory came flooding back. I fled.

"I've never told anyone of this. Not even Sarah. I've been thinking that perhaps I should tell Chief Schmertz — for the record. Mrs. Poplar is long dead. And they didn't have any children. But for the record. And I've been wondering, Detective Divine, if you'd be willing to advise me."

Tyler looked steadily at Farnsworth and realized that while he was talking she hadn't considered for a moment that he might not be telling the truth about how he had seen Malcolm James. Even though it now was clear that he had had Opportunity. She said, "What an extraordinary burden you've been harboring all these years, Mr. Lightfoot."

"Yes," Farnsworth said. "It's been a long time."

"If you wish, I'll accompany you to see Chief Schmertz."

"Would you?"

138

"Yes, of course. I'm certain you have nothing to fear. It's not as if you intentionally withheld evidence. You were confused, as any ten-year-old would have been."

Tyler said, "Come, we'd best go." As she stood she put a hand on Farnsworth's shoulder.

When they reached the Lightfoots' house, Tyler said she would call Farnsworth later in the day to set up a meeting with Chief Schmertz. Farnsworth thanked her, they shook hands, and Tyler left to keep her appointment with Maggie James.

Farnsworth stood on his porch and looked after Tyler. It was only then he realized that while talking to the detective he hadn't once stuttered, blushed, or mumbled into his lap. He had been very much in control. In the house, he met his sister who had returned from her lunch with Bettina and Webb and Jay. He said to her, "Do you have any idea where my tennis racquet is?"

TWENTY-SIX

Tyler and Maggie James sat in Hilary and Dru's parlor. Maggie had sobered up from the morning's mimosas, and, despite a dull headache, was thinking clearly. Her manner was neither bubbly, nor dour, nor fey. She said, "My husband is probably in Barbados."

Astonished, Tyler said, "Barbados?"

"That's where we were going directly from here. We always take a winter week there."

Still stunned, Tyler said, "But why didn't you tell us this before?"

"I wonder," Maggie said, her tone contemplative. "I suppose I just so badly wanted to believe he was really gone."

Tyler said nothing. Maggie continued: "I let my fantasies take over. And the alcohol didn't help. I've been drinking steadily since yesterday morning when you first came to interview us all." Maggie paused. "It's as if I've gone through a sea change this weekend — it's odd. I feel very strong now. I don't know if you've learned that my husband likes practical jokes. It seems I decided to play one on him for a change. Conjuring him gone. Now that I've returned to reality I suppose we should call the resort where we stay to see if he's arrived. It would be just like him."

Tyler agreed that they should call the resort immediately.

"Come with me, would you?" Maggie said. "I'm going to tell him I won't be joining him. I'd like you to be nearby when I do. Strong as I feel, I'm not accustomed to sea changes and I want to be firm. I'd like your support."

Maggie telephoned from the library and was told that Mr. James had not registered at the resort. Maggie asked to speak to the manager, who knew the Jameses well, and he told her yes, of course, he would tell Mr. James to telephone her at the Cape Gull number as soon as he arrived; he hoped everything was all right. The weather was just perfect for their stay.

During the silence that ensued after Maggie hung up, Tyler told herself that it really was time to call in Chief Schmertz. But first she would broach the subject of Maggie's disappearance during the treasure hunt.

141

Maggie was saying, "Damn him. He never makes things easy. Where is he?"

"There's something I have to ask you," Tyler said.

"Yes?" Maggie said, distracted.

"I wonder if you would tell me where you went on your way back from the treasure hunt?"

Maggie looked puzzled.

"The night of Hilary's dinner party, after the treasure hunt. When you left Drusilla Marx on Elm Street, and then joined her later."

"Oh!" Maggie said, welcoming something on which to concentrate. "I went back to the beach. We were walking back to the party. Dru was chattering away as she does, and I wasn't really listening I must admit. I was thinking about Malcolm and how I had seen him in a new light at the party. My talk with Bettina had penetrated deeply — do you know about our talk?" Tyler indicated that she didn't. "Well, before the party she and I talked for hours. About feminism. About patriarchy. About sexist husbands. A real eye-opener for me. I needed to think. So when Dru turned onto Elm — we were on Main Street — I veered off to the boardwalk where some benches overlook the sea. I just felt I needed to sit on one of those benches and look out to sea and be alone. But when I got there I began to feel chilled — just sitting, you know. So I left and went to catch up with Dru."

"The benches you're talking about aren't anywhere near the old fort, are they?"

"Oh no, they're right in town. The old fort is at the other end of the beach."

Tyler's thoughts went to Malcolm's encounter with Sterling in the dunes. Conceivably, their meeting could have taken place just about the time Maggie was sitting on the town bench looking out to sea — if Maggie was

142

telling the truth. How was she going to tell Maggie about what Sterling had told her? And should she even do so if Malcolm was perhaps only off in Barbados somewhere and shortly would call his wife to join him? Tyler needed some time to think. But first she had to tell Maggie of Farnsworth having seen Malcolm lying in the sand, which she proceeded to do.

"Really?" Maggie responded. "Well, he *was* drunk. I'd agree with Farnsworth that he probably was just passed out. How strange. What do you make of it?"

"I think you should consider calling in Chief Schmertz. Now that we have Farnsworth's disclosure and yours about Barbados, perhaps we should consider more seriously the possibility that something untoward has happened to Mr. James."

Maggie was quiet for a while. Then she said, "I really don't know what to do. My instinct tells me he's all right. He's due back at work next Monday, a week from tomorrow."

Tyler said she thought that waiting a week was not a good idea.

"I suppose you're right," Maggie said. "But I really feel he's okay. I should ask Hilary what she thinks. Let's at least wait until morning. People come to their senses on Monday mornings."

TWENTY-SEVEN

Monday

At one p.m., Malcolm having not surfaced, Maggie James, after consulting with Hilary, called Detective Divine. She asked her to contact Chief Schmertz, who, after debriefing Tyler, set in motion a police investigation. Malcolm James was declared an official Missing Person.

* * * * *

Later that afternoon Tyler and Nina were in the Pink Tea Cup waiting for Agatha Junior to arrive with their tea.

"It's been more difficult than I thought," Nina was saying. "When Content left yesterday afternoon I was determined that that was that. I still am, but she's telephoned half a dozen times. She refuses to accept it."

Tyler nodded.

"You're wonderful, do you know that?"

Tyler smiled.

"She's coming back tomorrow," Nina said. Chief Schmertz wants to talk to her. And I've asked her to pick up her things. I dread it. She has an amazing ability to turn things on their heads, to make you think you're the crazy one — if you're susceptible to that sort of thing. As I, unfortunately, have been."

Tyler still listened in silence. She knew Nina had to talk.

"Content told me you were having an affair with Bettina."

"What?" Tyler exclaimed, breaking her silence. "For heaven's sake."

Nina was smiling. "True. She showed me Bettina's 'Sisters Unite' button which she found on the hallway floor."

Tyler laughed. "It must have been lying in the hallway all day. I didn't have it when I got home yesterday morning. I assumed you'd found it in the bedroom."

"It having fallen off during our crazy morning," Nina teased. She was silent for a moment. Then she said, "Listen, I'm going to say something incredibly risky. I'm going to say that I think I'm falling in love with you."

"Isn't that odd," Tyler said. "I've wanted to say those very words ever since we sat down."

145

"And we haven't even slept together."

"Oh, but we have. How soon they forget."

Nina laughed. "What a great memory we already have of our first night together."

"A truly memorable occasion. Especially Sterling Sunday morning being so seriously helpful — with no clothes on."

"I really do love him."

"I know."

"He just can't seem to find someone special."

"Lots of people can't."

"True." Nina toyed with her napkin. "You know, I once had a brief affair with someone who kept saying, over and over: You're a special person. Over and over she said it. Then I learned she was saying those very words to three other women at the same time. She was a collector. A master. I never met anyone like that. It was quite a sobering experience."

"A charitable thought would be that she thinks all women are special."

"That certainly is kind."

They smiled.

"After I got over the shock of her, after the revulsion, I felt sorry for her. She lives without intimacy. Tyler?"

"Yes?"

"Do you think our falling in love will grow into love?"

"Oh my. And in broad daylight. I'd like to say I haven't a doubt in the world. But at our ages I think we know better than that. First, we have to celebrate the in love. Then, later, the real work starts."

"I can hardly wait. Why don't we just skip the first step?"

"And miss all those ringing bells and rainbows? Never!"

"Bells and rainbows?"

"No question."

"We could combine step one and step two."

"Now there's a thought."

Agatha Junior, smiling beatifically, arrived with the tea. "You two look great," she said.

TWENTY-EIGHT

Tuesday

Late in the afternoon Nina telephoned Tyler to say that Content, after several phone arguments, had postponed her trip to Cape Gull until Saturday. "I don't know what she's up to. I don't like it, but I can't force her to come. I don't know how Chief Schmertz is handling it." She paused. "Do you think we should meet? I'm feeling we should wait until all this is over. My anxiety level is not terribly attractive. I want to come to you whole."

"I think that may be wise," Tyler conceded. "And it might not be a good idea to phone. I'd want to see you. Actually, I've been doing some thinking. I have some things I want to look into in New York. This is probably a good time to go. Chief Schmertz has the Malcolm investigation pretty much in hand."

"What have you been thinking about?" Nina asked.

"Oh, about disrupted lives . . . and journalists and detectives. I'll save the details for when we meet."

"I miss you already. Don't you dare go dancing in New York!" Nina laughed. "Listen to me! Possessivemania. Forgive me?"

"It's nice, in one way."

"Not in another."

"Agreed."

"Our first agreement. Nice! Will you be back by Saturday?"

"That is an insecure question," Tyler said. "The extravagantly romantic answer is: Even if I have to move mountains."

"That is a security-inducing answer," Nina said. "I'll call you on Saturday as soon as Content leaves. Take good care of yourself until then."

"And you."

After fixing herself a cup of tea, Tyler's thoughts abruptly returned to the fact that Content Beebe had postponed her interview with Chief Schmertz until Saturday. She sighed, and went into her study to concentrate.

149

As she tried to reconstruct her interview with Content, one question lingered: Why hadn't Content seen Malcolm lying in the dunes? Had Malcolm gone off before she got there? Assuming, again, that Sterling and Farnsworth were telling the truth? Dunes! Of course. She reached for the phone to telephone Chief Schmertz, but stopped. She was not unaware that her objectivity about Content Beebe was sorely frayed. However, she said to herself, reaching again for the phone, the entire matter could be cleared up with one question to Content: Did you see Malcolm James lying in the *dunes* when you exited the fort? And how would Content answer? Would she continue to lie — if she was lying? One step at a time, Tyler decided. She dialed Chief Schmertz's number.

TWENTY-NINE

Saturday
Still Cape Gull
Still January
Still 1975

Dearhearts!

  *Please, please forgive me for not writing since Sunday
last. Almost a week! There are really only two reasons why*

people who like to write letters (as I do) don't — (1) they're depressed or (2) they're having an affair. Well — I'm not depressed. More of the latter later.

First, about the murder — which we still don't really know is a murder. The supposed deceased has not surfaced and is now (has been all week) an official Missing Person. The cops have taken over, with Detective Tyler Divine as consultant. Wife Maggie has gone home to Philadelphia — a changed woman. I wrote you about my talk with her. Isn't it continually amazing how quickly, with just the tiniest bit of prompting, women recognize their oppression? She had to stay drunk for the better part of two days to process it — but what a breakthrough! Her energy level vis-à-vis her life, her own life, is vibrating all over the place. Praise be!

But the main news here is that tonight, in approximately one hour's time, Cape Gull will be the setting for what I am certain is a first — its very own consciousness raising evening. We've billed it as a book discussion (my book), but that's only the bait. It's going to be weird doing CR with gay men. Not to mention other CR no-nos, like sisters and lovers. Goddess knows what it will be like. I can hardly wait.

You're probably wondering if I'm ever coming home. I will, of course, and soon. Time magazine has found me (thanks for not telling them where I was). It was my mother's doing. She and her Bulgarian (did I tell you about him?) were in Hong Kong at some spiffy party and Mother was blathering away about "my youngest" (me) "the famous writer," and she was overheard by Time's Man in the Orient, who, apparently, rushed to his Telex. They hated getting scooped by People. It must have been like your son running off with your mistress. Ah vanitas! You'd think Time would have better things to do — like

finding out what really happened to Martha Mitchell, par
example. *Too bad* Life *is gone. I would have loved jumping
for Philippe Halsman.*

*You will never guess what I'm about to do. Take a
bubble bath, that's what. My sister has this incredible solid
copper bathtub overlaid with periwinkle blue enamel —
and it's big enough to accommodate three. And my
sister-in-law Hilary, yes, I guess she is my sister-in-law,
has this gorgeous bubble bath in this gorgeous jar
imported from Switzerland. Talk about privilege. My
dears! And don't start in about my trust fund; as you well
know, it's taken me many young years (with your help) to
deal intelligently with it myself. Potter, Potter, Potter and
Kline have not yet recovered from my coming of age.
Onward!*

*I won't sign off, for I intend to continue this letter after
tonight's gathering, and I fully believe it'll be one for the
archives. Hilary's main concern about tonight is whether
to serve coffee or hot cocoa. "Bettina, dear," she asked me,
"what does one serve at a book discussion?" I didn't tell
her: herself.*

Ciao caras — *more anon.*

THIRTY

Hilary had turned on every lamp in the parlor and had arranged fresh flowers everywhere. Bettina said to herself: You'd think we were going to be filmed. Already assembled were: Nina, Sterling, Webb, Jay, Dru, Hilary, and Bettina. No one outside of their circle had accepted the invitation to the gathering. Some said they might come, and took down the address. But so far — no strange faces. And it was time to begin.

Bettina and Jay had consulted earlier and had decided that Bettina would facilitate. "Would everyone please find seats," she said now.

Hilary thought: Thank goodness for well-furnished Victorian parlors. There were seats aplenty. She fussed finding places for all.

"Sit down, Hilary," Bettina said. "Everyone here is quite capable of finding her or his own space."

"I was just . . . " Hilary said, but Bettina said, "Sit down."

Hilary obeyed.

With everyone seated, Bettina said, "Now, will all lovers who are sitting next to each other split up." Everyone looked at Hilary and Dru. Dru nervously changed places with Sterling. Webb and Jay were already separated by Nina.

"Good," Bettina said. She was sitting next to Webb.

"My," Hilary said lightly, "we look like a seance."

"Do we?" Bettina said. "Would you care to elaborate on that?"

"It was merely a pleasantry," Hilary said.

"Would you care to define pleasantry?" Bettina said.

"Why no, no I wouldn't." Hilary became silent.

"Good," Bettina said. "Let's begin. First, we're breaking every single rule of classic consciousness raising."

"Consciousness raising?" Hilary and Dru said simultaneously.

"Yes," Bettina said.

"But I was under the impression we were going to discuss your book," Hilary said.

Jay interrupted. "We will, in the course of the evening. It's all of a piece."

155

"Fine with me," Sterling said.

Nina and Webb nodded in agreement.

Dru looked at Hilary before she said, "Sure, okay with me. Hil?"

"Well, if the group agrees."

"No," Bettina said. "You, Hilary. What about you?"

Hilary looked at her friends, who were looking at her. She thought: Goodness! And said, "Well, yes, yes, all right. But I have never done such a thing."

Nina laughed. "You're hardly alone in that. Come on, Hil, you're among friends."

"Right," Dru said.

Hilary, somewhat reassured, managed a small smile.

Dru said, "Go to it, Sis."

"The purpose is to talk," Bettina said. "And the point is to be honest. Save the chitchat and the pleasantries for a cocktail party." She paused. "I'm not sure how this is going to work. One of the rules is no lovers in the same group . . . " She looked at Hilary and Dru, and Webb and Jay. "And the fact that we're women and men together is weird. But let's give it a try. After this short preamble I'm going to fade out as the facilitator and join in as one of the group. But I'll mostly be silent. This is your night." She said intently, "Our jobs are to listen to each other, to allow each other whatever time and space desired — to accept, maybe to connect, to judge nothing, and in turn to talk ourselves. So, let's begin by going around the room, and everyone just introduce her or himself."

"But we all know each other, surely," Hilary said.

"Do we?" Bettina said.

No one spoke.

Bettina said, "So, whoever wants to start, start."

Still no one spoke.

156

After a while: "I'll begin." It was Nina. "But where?" she added. Everyone smiled and shifted in their seats. "All right," Nina continued. "I'm Nina Petrovich. I spell my name with an 'h.' Actually, there shouldn't be an 'h.' However, if there weren't, the 'c' would be hard, when it's really soft. My father couldn't stand the 'ick' sound. Made him feel like he didn't know who he was. Thus the 'h,' to make it easier for Americans. Americans are so language-poor. As if the rest of the world didn't exist — except in relation to them . . . us. We're so ready to turn everyone into ourselves — to think in terms of 'the other.' I've always related to that concept." She looked around the room.

"We were 'the other' in spades — my family. Most of you know my parents were old lefties who didn't opt for the certainty of the American Dream. Picture this: a Midwest immigrant neighborhood. A two-story house in a row of ethnic houses. And instead of Jesus . . . " Nina stopped and said to Bettina, "Is this all right?"

"There's no right here," Bettina said, folding her arms across her chest full of activist buttons.

Nina nodded. But before she could resume, the doorbell rang.

"Latecomer," Jay said, getting up. "I'll get it."

When he returned to the parlor, Hilary said, "Why Detective Divine! What . . . we . . . is it about Malcolm?"

Tyler looked around the room, nodding greetings and smiling at Nina. "No," she said to Hilary. "It isn't about Mr. James. I've come for the discussion. Sorry to be late. I was detained in New York."

Hilary and Dru raised eyebrows at each other.

"Welcome!" Bettina said. "We've just begun."

Tyler found herself a seat, and Nina resumed.

157

"I've just been talking about my family," she said. "And Simone de Beauvoir's concept of 'the other' — at least that's where I first read about it." She shrugged. "Instead of Jesus hanging on our wall — as he did all up and down our ethnic street — we had a photograph of Karl Marx above my father's desk in the living room. And on the desk a huge old heavy copy of *Das Kapital*. Sort of like a family Bible. I still can sing the *Internationale: Stand up ye wretched slaves of labor* . . . or something like that." When she spoke again, her voice had changed; it was softer. "It's odd," she said. "What's really whirling around in my head is not my family at all. What I really want to tell you is that Content and I . . . well, we've come to the end of the road."

Hilary's lips formed a silent O, and she was trying to get Dru's attention. Nina was looking at Tyler.

"It's not been easy," Nina continued. Then she stopped. "Now that I've told you . . . " She stopped again, and turned to Bettina.

"It's all right to pass," Bettina said. Nina decided to.

After a bit Jay spoke up. "My father was in the Merchant Marine at the beginning of World War Two — he was a cook on ships. They called him Jew boy. And he used to laugh. One did in those days. We were only 'sort of' Jewish. We weren't religious — and we identified culturally only when my grandparents were around." Jay scratched in his beard. "But when I got to Harvard I identified like crazy. Like when I first met Webb — the very first thing I told him was that I was Jewish. It was as if I was saying to him: Okay, go ahead, just you dare to make an anti-Semitic remark, even a nuance, Mr. Webster Thatcher the third." Jay smiled fondly at his lover. "I became so prejudiced against WASPs. And there I was, about to sleep with one. I'd put them all in one big barrel.

158

I had decided that they didn't know how to eat, or joke, or laugh. I'll never forget the first real WASP dinner I went to. In New York. I had gone with my college roommate to his parents' house for a weekend. On each plate there was one little sliver of veal, maybe ten peas, no gravy, no bread. And for dessert, a tablespoon of vanilla ice cream and a teaspoon of chocolate sauce. After dinner I went out for cigarettes, and I stopped at a deli for the biggest pastrami on pumpernickel you've ever seen, dripping in grease — and pickled green tomatoes, and, well, you get the picture." Everyone was smiling. "Anyway," Jay continued, addressing Nina, "I just wanted to say that I connect to what you've said."

Dru cleared her throat. Bettina thought: Brava, Sis.

"My parents divorced when I was just a kid. My mother started running around Europe with me in tow, acting as if she were some sort of countess. Countess Marx. We lived in all these incredible baroque hotels in one country after another. I used to jump rope in the hallways. For a while I thought I was Liechtensteinian. I didn't know who I was. I was 'the other' wherever we were." Hilary's great-grandmother's grandfather clock chimed, then continued its methodical ticking. Dru did not continue.

"I was valedictorian of my high school class — and I wrote poetry — and I didn't play sports." Webb adjusted his spectacles. "I always felt out of step. I didn't have many friends — except for Sam — he was Mr. Jocko then — but we were friends. Things got better in college. There were other guys there who were super smart, who wrote poetry, who didn't play sports. We were all, our bunch, out of step." Webb stopped and indicated he'd pass for now.

159

Sterling shifted in his seat. "This is very interesting," he said. "Does it occur to anyone that we've been talking about the concept of 'the other' for four rounds now, and no one who has spoken has mentioned that most profound otherness of which we are all a part — our homosexuality." He looked around the room.

Hilary sat up straighter in her chair.

Bettina thought: Finally!

Sterling was about to continue, but again the doorbell rang.

"For goodness sake," Hilary said.

"I'll go," Dru said. She returned with eyebrows raised and walked to Hilary's side. A second later, Farnsworth entered the parlor, followed by a tall, broad-shouldered man.

"Sam!" Webb said, jumping up. "Sam!"

"Farnsworth!" Hilary said, also getting up. "Dru! Farnsworth!" She turned to the man Webb had called Sam. "How do you do? I am Hilary James."

"Sam Cake. We've met."

Most everyone was standing now. Bettina walked over to Sam. "Samantha?" she said. "Your hair, where's your hair?"

"In the wig box," Sam said.

Hilary carefully lowered herself into her chair. Farnsworth! she said to herself. She pulled at Dru's jacket hem and whispered, "Dru, it's Farnsworth."

"Yes," Dru said. "So it certainly seems." She was smiling widely now.

Once Sam had found a seat, he said, "Sorry we're late. I was hoping Farnsworth would have gone on without me. Hope we're not interrupting too badly."

"Not in the least," Jay said. "I'm crazy happy you're here . . . what happened to Joan Crawford?"

160

Sam looked fondly at Farnsworth, who had walked over to say hello to Tyler. "I've had a change of heart," Sam said.

"Okay!" Jay said. "Welcome!"

Farnsworth was greeting Tyler, "So nice to see you, Detective Divine."

Tyler held out her hand. "The feeling is mutual, Mr. Lightfoot."

Nina walked over to Tyler and embraced her, whispering in her ear, "I'm so glad you're here."

Hilary's eyes were on sticks.

Sterling called for quiet. "All right," he said, "let's settle down. I was just beginning something profound."

Farnsworth and Sam's entrance had enlivened everyone save for Hilary, who looked comatose. Everyone was smiling and talking. Before their arrival the meeting had begun to feel very funereal — normal for a first time, Bettina knew. Now, she thought, rubbing her hands together: Bingo!

Sterling was still waiting for quiet. Everyone settled into seats. He resumed. "As I was saying, here we all are, homosexuals . . . no, let me rephrase that, gay men and lesbians." He paused. "No, let me rephrase *that* — lesbians and gay men." He nodded to Bettina. She nodded back.

Hilary found her voice. "But Detective Divine . . . "

"We don't interrupt each other," Bettina said. "An important rule."

Tyler spoke up. "As Sterling was saying, here we all are, lesbians and gay men."

Hilary put a hand to her forehead and returned to catatonia. Dru was sitting on the edge of her chair, still smiling widely.

"Yes," Sterling said, "thank you."

But again the doorbell rang.

"This is unbelievable," Dru said.

Bettina went to answer. She returned, holding Sarah Lightfoot's hand.

"Sarah!" Farnsworth said, jumping to his feet.

"Farnsworth!" Sarah said.

They walked toward each other and embraced.

"I fear I am going to faint," Hilary uttered.

"Don't you dare faint," Bettina said, rushing to Hilary's side. "You haven't spoken yet."

"Another chair!" Sterling was shouting. "Another chair!"

Hilary didn't move.

"I'll find one," Webb said. When he passed Sam, he hugged him. "Son of a gun! Son of a gun! Fantastic!"

When Webb returned with a chair for Sarah, Sterling said, "Ladies and gentlemen, women and men, if the doorbell rings yet once again ... "

"We'll just get another chair," Bettina said.

When everyone had calmed down, Sterling resumed. "For our recent arrivals — we've been talking of the concept of 'the other.' My point is that no one who has spoken has mentioned the profound otherness of being lesbian or gay. It's the one thing those of us in the closet don't talk about, even among ourselves — serious talk, that is. We just go blithely along as if it were extraneous. I, for instance, could go on and on about the otherness of being a writer, especially during all those years when I was struggling, writing books whose shelf life was two months — and then into the warehouse shredder. It's taken many years to become the so-called famous writer I seem to have become. But I still think of myself as this outsider — in the manner of people who once were fat and now are thin, thinking they are still fat. I have an image

162

now: acerbic expatriate American writer. And that image is totally bereft of my essence: I am a gay man.

"I can just see Wystan turning over in his grave. His argument was that an author's emotional self belongs in the realm of things private, has nothing to do with his or her work. I used to think that . . . but I'm beginning to change my mind. In fact, I'm almost prepared to say that Mr. Auden was wrong. My love life is not an irrelevant issue. It informs my work. It is, in fact, my essence." He smiled. "Well, I've gone on too long. I'll stop. Not that I don't have more to say. In fact, a new book idea about essences is beginning to percolate, yes . . . but I'll yield for now."

"Essence is so very apt," Tyler said, looking at Sterling. Others nodded in agreement. Tyler looked at Nina and continued.

"I recently went through something I hope no one in this room ever has to experience." She paused. "My lover died a year ago." Again she paused. "She was murdered. You undoubtedly saw the press reports. The papers were beside themselves. Kimberly Green?"

Hilary's mouth dropped open. Others were equally stunned.

"We were together ten years. No one really knew. Friends, of course, did. Others suspected, I suppose. But we were experts at confusing matters. There were men around all the time, so-called dates. Gay men. We helped them, too, in their subterfuge. I was working as a reporter then. So when Kim and I were in public together I always had my reporter's credentials to cloak things. Kim was on the West Coast a lot, or traveling, filming. My base was New York City. But we shared a country house in East Hampton.

"You must have read about the mugging. She was on her way to my apartment in New York. But what you didn't read about was how I wasn't allowed into the emergency room at the hospital. I wasn't at her side when she died. Only blood relatives and spouses could gain entrance. I was officially neither. And at the funeral I went as a reporter. Her family didn't know I existed . . . ten years. Then she was gone. There was no acceptable way for me to mourn. I thought I would suffocate. Kim's essence . . . my essence . . . they didn't exist.

"After the funeral I left my job and went to France. I was paralyzed with anger. Anger at muggers, at the press's hounding . . . at myself for having lived a lie for so long . . . at Kim for having done the same . . . at Kim for dying. At the pressures that had forced us into such an existence. When I returned I felt lost. There's a continuity in being officially widowed. Painful as it is, it is something. A cultural given that allows one to mourn with dignity. To deal with all the various angers. I was so at sea.

"I just disappeared from what had been my life. I would catch muggers, I thought, I'd do that much. There might be some solace in that. It was a rash step — I just did it. I ran. And it's never felt right. It's been just another type of closet. And I haven't even caught any muggers."

Tyler looked at Nina. "I suppose what I'm saying is that we need to stop the hiding."

During the ensuing silence Bettina knew it would be difficult for anyone to speak for a while. It was always thus at some point during CR. Overwhelming things emerged.

It was Farnsworth — he who seldom talked — who broke the silence. "I just want to thank Detective Divine

164

— Tyler — and support what she said about stopping the hiding. There are degrees of the closet. Mine all but killed me."

He looked at Sam. "That's all I'll say for now."

Sam spoke up. "If I may . . . you all know what I've recently been about. I've done nothing all week but examine why I felt so strongly that only by becoming a transsexual would I find some peace. I read a very interesting book this week — the author played tight end for a professional football team. I played that position in college. He writes about how he hated himself for years because he got turned on by his teammates, some of them, and he dealt with it by drinking himself silly most nights. It's the first time a professional athlete has come out. I'm beginning to think my desire to become a transsexual was my way of avoiding being a gay man — and all that that implies. I'm not saying other transsexuals had my dynamic. No, I can't say that. Just as there are homosexualities — all sorts of variations on the theme — surely there must be transsexualities. I had never fallen in love with a man. That was a very large no-no for jocks. I just fucked. Sorry Hilary. Somehow a quick fuck was okay. And living as a gay man was not. Well, I've changed my mind."

Sam smiled at Farnsworth, who did not blush.

Bettina looked at Sarah.

"I don't know what to say," Sarah said. "This is all very new to me. All I know is, I feel absolutely splendid! And I'm so pleased to be here with you. I'm certain I'll have a good deal to say next time we meet."

Everyone turned their attention to Hilary.

Hilary adjusted her chiffon neck scarf and picked some lint from her trouser leg. Then she said, "With all due respect to those who have spoken, I have *never* felt like

165

'the other.' " She paused. "Only once, perhaps, at my coming out . . . I mean to say, my debut. It was at the Bellevue-Stratford. I was tall for a young woman, and in my white gown and high pumps I veritably towered. I remember the occasion as one of extreme awkwardness. The young men with whom I danced, almost all of whom reeked of liquor, came to my shoulder. I did experience a sense of odd woman out then — but that was merely adolescence."

Hilary looked as if she was not going to continue. Then she did. "Actually," she said, "there *was* another time. It was when I was at Vassar. I had one of those normal schoolgirl crushes on my golf instructor. Miss Meaker. She was exceedingly sturdy in build, taller than I, and I used to stare in wonder at the way she spoke. She barely moved her lips. I followed her around rather like a puppy dog — a rather large puppy dog, I do concede." Hilary smiled a small smile. "I was exceedingly happy. But I did come to notice that whenever there were other girls around, my classmates, they giggled and whispered to each other. I do concede that then, yes, I did experience a feeling of otherness — but, again, that was during my youth. As an adult . . .

"Well, there was that time in Martinique — you remember, Dru. We were staying at a rather posh resort. People dressed for dinner. It was a small, intimate hotel — actually a series of quaint thatched cottages. We took our meals in the main edifice. The first evening I had gone on ahead to cocktails before dinner. Dru had taken a late swim and was still dressing. I was having a marvelous talk about Philadelphia with a thin gentleman who was wearing a foulard. He lived on the Main Line. However, the moment Dru joined us his manner, which had been quite jolly, became guarded. He excused himself and went

166

off in search of his wife. And then I noticed that everyone was coupled off — middle-aged husbands and wives, the women in cocktail dresses. Dru and I wore trousers, lovely resort wear in bright colors — it was a resort — but nonetheless we did stand out as different from those assembled. We circulated during the cocktails . . . I do enjoy light conversation. But we encountered a certain reticence. I was perplexed. And for the rest of our stay no one went out of their way to approach us for an excursion or a chat by the pool. It was I who always made the overtures and in several cases was rather rudely dispensed with. Dru and I decided that henceforth we would take our winter weeks at larger, more heterogeneous resorts. One simply makes accommodations. One can live a perfectly lovely life without being obvious."

Bettina was shaking her head. She badly wanted to talk. Fuck it, she thought. "Hilary, I'm now going to break the rules. Have you ever said the word lesbian in your life? Or gay? Or even homosexual?"

"That's not fair, Betts," Dru said. "You're interrupting."

Bettina apologized. "You're right. I'm sorry. You're right. Even those of us who are invariably politically correct sometimes aren't."

Sarah spoke up. "I know those resorts, Hilary. Farnsworth and I have gone to them. We're always taken for husband and wife and when it becomes clear that we're actually brother and sister, we've gotten the oddest looks. At those places legitimacy is granted only to those who are married . . . and preferably in an Episcopal Church." Bettina laughed. Sarah continued, "The only way I enjoyed myself at those resorts was on the tennis courts. One swings a racquet uncoupled."

167

"Just think of all the ways to be coupled," Nina said. "Brother and sister. Sisters. Mother and daughter. Friends. Colleagues. Cousins. On and on."

"There *was* another time," Hilary was saying. Everyone turned to look at her.

"At Mother's funeral. I wanted Dru with me, of course. Malcolm was not at his best that day. I was faring reasonably well, nary a tear, until the minister mentioned Mother's garden. His wife, a dear friend of Mother's, obviously had coached him. He was describing Mother's various flower beds in great detail, naming flower after flower, in a rather splendid poetic flow, and I simply . . . I simply collapsed into sobs, reaching past Malcolm's shoulders — he was sitting next to me — to the pew behind for Dru's hand . . . "

A voice came from the parlor's doorway. "And I told you to control yourself. To behave yourself."

Malcolm James walked into the parlor.

"Malcolm!" Hilary cried out.

Everyone else sat stunned.

Malcolm's left arm was in a sling and there was a gauzy bandage over his right eye. "Forgive the melodramatic entrance," he said.

Something's wrong, Bettina thought. Aside from the bandages.

No part of Malcolm James's anatomy was moving. He was not bouncing up and down on the balls of his feet, his good arm was at his side, his head was not bobbing; he stood amazingly still. And he was talking slowly — not out of the corner of his mouth.

"But look at you!" Hilary said. "What in heaven's name happened? Are you all right?"

Sterling rose and offered Malcolm his chair.

"Thanks," Malcolm said, offering his hand. As he sat, he and Sterling shook hands. He looked around the room. "I owe you all an apology." His eyes rested on Tyler. "You must be Detective Divine. Maggie told me about you."

"Maggie?" Dru interrupted. "You've seen Maggie?"

"I was with her all day. She told me you were meeting here tonight."

"But where in the world have you been?" Hilary demanded. "And what in the world happened to you?"

Malcolm breathed with difficulty. It was obvious he was in pain. "I was in New York," he said.

"New York?" Dru said.

"Yes."

"But, but ... "

"Don't, Hilary. I've come to apologize."

"Have you been listening at the door?" Dru said.

"For a while. I was sitting in the kitchen. I let myself in the back door."

"Now that's really shitty."

"Please, Dru. I wanted to join you. It's about time I did."

Hilary gasped.

Oh wow! Bettina thought.

Hilary, her voice high and thin, said, "Perhaps it is time to serve the hot cocoa."

"This is precisely not the time to serve hot cocoa, Hilary," Bettina said.

"Thanks," Malcolm said, turning his attention to Bettina. "I read your book while I was in New York. I read a lot of books."

Bettina was thinking: Wonder of fucking wonders.

"You said you talked to Maggie," Dru said. "Why didn't you call her? We all thought you were dead ... well, some of us did."

Malcolm sighed and ran his good hand through his hair. "You're right, I should have. But I needed to be disconnected. I needed to concentrate on myself."

Bettina realized that that was exactly what Maggie had done — gone off into an alcoholic distancing to process her own sea change.

"I spent all of today with Maggie," Malcolm continued. "The first thing she said was she wanted a divorce. As it should be. For both our sakes. I'm gay, Dru. I'm a gay man. I've always been gay."

"But, but . . . " Hilary said.

"But I've always hated homosexuals," Malcolm finished for her. "True. Myself included. I couldn't accept it. And never did anything about it. Just hated it." Malcolm looked at Sterling.

Sterling said, "But how did you get hurt?"

"I got beat up."

Hilary shuddered.

Malcolm looked around the room. "It might help to talk about it."

"Oh Malcolm," Hilary said.

"Please, Hilary. I've come to apologize — especially to you. I had forgotten about Mother's funeral. Dru *should* have been sitting with us, in the family pew. And I apologize to everyone else. Maggie told me what I've put you through. I stopped in at Chief Schmertz's before coming here." He looked at Tyler and said to her, "I'm sorry you're out of a job now."

Tyler nodded. "The pleasure is all mine, Mr. James. I'm sure we're all relieved you've returned."

"Indeed," Sterling said.

Everyone was silent for a long while. Then Malcolm spoke.

170

"I was walking on Central Park West and passed a bench where a guy was sitting. I looked at him, passed by, and he got up and followed me. I slowed down at an entrance to the park and we turned into it together. When we got to a secluded spot he reached for me . . . and then he socked me. And then two other guys appeared. I was off guard. I fell and they were at me. I never got a punch in. I lost consciousness. When I came to, someone was standing over me. I was scared, but this young man helped me up. And helped me to a cab. He stayed with me in the emergency room of the hospital. Afterward he took me home with him."

Malcolm turned to Bettina and said, "He turned out to be a gay activist."

Bettina's young feminist heart skipped a beat.

Malcolm continued, "I spent the week in his apartment, going through his bookshelves. And when he got home from work we talked — or I should say he talked to me. Young guy, in his early thirties. He was so great." Malcolm looked into his lap. When he lifted his eyes he was smiling painfully. "He was so free."

Dru felt tears coming; she stemmed them. Nina and Tyler were looking at each other. Hilary was staring at her brother. No one spoke.

After a while Sterling walked over to Malcolm and put his hands on his shoulders. He said, "Perhaps it's not time for hot cocoa, but I think we could use a break. I certainly could use a drink."

Malcolm lifted his good arm and put his hand over Sterling's. Dru let her tears come. Bettina gave a passing thought to miracles.

Then Bettina said she thought a break was a good idea. She looked at Jay, who had his arm around Webb.

171

"Absolutely," Jay said, standing. "Cape Gull's very first historical CR group is declared officially recessed."

"And when we reassemble," Sterling said, "we will discuss — using Bettina's book as text — how by our very existence we threaten the narrow-minded moral, social, and yes, even, political order . . . examining carefully the homophobic, sexist, heterosexist, racist, and classist status quo."

Bettina beamed.

"Oh my goodness," Hilary said. She turned to Sarah Lightfoot. "There's also hot cocoa, dear."

"Scotch for me," Sarah said. She embraced Bettina. Over Sarah's shoulder, Bettina winked at her sister. Dru winked back.

Jay and Webb walked over to talk to Sam and Farnsworth. "How did you know we were here?" Webb asked. "Sarah," Farnsworth said. "She mentioned it yesterday, in passing. So I called Sam and we decided we would go. I told him to meet me at the Pink Tea Cup. I thought it might be a good way to gather strength to bring Sam home to Sarah." He smiled. "And then she walked in." They all smiled.

Nearby, Nina and Tyler were talking.

"Content's really gone?" Tyler was saying.

"Just before I left for here. I called you, but got your service. I wanted you to be here."

"We have Bettina to thank. She tracked me down in New York." She paused. "Was it very awful?"

"It always is, isn't it? Emerging from denial. Content never wanted to do the real work. And I just continued, complainingly, stuck in fantasyland. It was never a good relationship, we're both better off. You were lucky to have had Kim."

"Kim's gone," Tyler said.

"So is Content."

The women looked at each other.

"Well, then," Nina said, "there's no reason in the world, Detective Divine, why we can't dine together tomorrow night."

"No reason at all," Tyler said. "I'll cook."

They embraced and walked to join Sterling and Malcolm.

In the kitchen, emptying ice trays, Hilary said to Dru, "You know, darling, there *was* that other time . . . "

In the parlor Bettina stood quietly next to Hilary's great-grandmother's grandfather clock. "You know, Sappho," she said, looking fondly around the room at her new friends, "they may begin to know what they're doing after all."

Oddly, Sappho replied. She said: Wouldn't that be lovely. Let's wish them goddess-speed.

ACKNOWLEDGEMENTS

For long term kindnesses, both emotional and practical, I thank Marilyn Lamkay, Jean Millar, Frederica Leser, Marijane Meaker, Barbara Ulrich, Ann Stokes, Sandy Rapp, Jonathan Silin, Joan Hamilton, and my East Hampton writing group: Irene Gould, James Haigney, and Zoe Kamitses. For more recent love and support, my thanks to Lynn Martin, Deborah Perry, Lise Weil, and especially, Pat Maravel.

Finally, bouquets to Katherine V. Forrest for her sensitive editing skills.

ABOUT THE AUTHOR

Dolores Klaich, writer, editor, and longtime lesbian/gay and feminist activist, is currently working as an AIDS educator for the Long Island Association for Aids Care, Inc. She is the author of *Woman Plus Woman: Attitudes Toward Lesbianism*, to be reprinted by Naiad Press early in 1989 in a fifteenth anniversary edition.

A few of the publications of
THE NAIAD PRESS, INC.
P.O. Box 10543 ● Tallahassee, Florida 32302
Phone (904) 539-9322
Mail orders welcome. Please include 15% postage.

HEAVY GILT by Dolores Klaich. 192 pp. Lesbian detective/
disappearing homophobes/upper class gay society.
ISBN 0-941483-25-8 $8.95

DOUBLE DAUGHTER by Vicki P. McConnell. 216 pp. A Nyla
Wade Mystery, third in the series.   ISBN 0-941483-26-6   8.95

THE FINER GRAIN by Denise Ohio. 216 pp. Brilliant young
college lesbian novel.   ISBN 0-941483-11-8   8.95

THE AMAZON TRAIL by Lee Lynch. 216 pp. Life, travel & lore
of famous lesbian author.   ISBN 0-941483-27-4   8.95

HIGH CONTRAST by Jessie Lattimore. 264 pp. Women of the
Crystal Palace.   ISBN 0-941483-17-7   8.95

OCTOBER OBSESSION by Meredith More. Josie's rich, secret
Lesbian life.   ISBN 0-941483-18-5   8.95

LESBIAN CROSSROADS by Ruth Baetz. 276 pp. Contemporary
Lesbian lives.   ISBN 0-941483-21-5   9.95

BEFORE STONEWALL: THE MAKING OF A GAY AND
LESBIAN COMMUNITY by Andrea Weiss & Greta Schiller.
96 pp., 25 illus.   ISBN 0-941483-20-7   7.95

WE WALK THE BACK OF THE TIGER by Patricia A. Murphy.
192 pp. Romantic Lesbian novel/beginning women's movement.
ISBN 0-941483-13-4   8.95

SUNDAY'S CHILD by Joyce Bright. 216 pp. Lesbian athletics, at
last the novel about sports.   ISBN 0-941483-12-6   8.95

OSTEN'S BAY by Zenobia N. Vole. 204 pp. Sizzling adventure
romance set on Bonaire.   ISBN 0-941483-15-0   8.95

LESSONS IN MURDER by Claire McNab. 216 pp. 1st in a stylish
mystery series.   ISBN 0-941483-14-2   8.95

YELLOWTHROAT by Penny Hayes. 240 pp. Margarita, bandit,
kidnaps Julia.   ISBN 0-941483-10-X   8.95

SAPPHISTRY: THE BOOK OF LESBIAN SEXUALITY by
Pat Califia. 3d edition, revised. 208 pp.   ISBN 0-941483-24-X   8.95

CHERISHED LOVE by Evelyn Kennedy. 192 pp. Erotic
Lesbian love story.   ISBN 0-941483-08-8   8.95

LAST SEPTEMBER by Helen R. Hull. 208 pp. Six stories & a
glorious novella.   ISBN 0-941483-09-6   8.95

THE SECRET IN THE BIRD by Camarin Grae. 312 pp. Striking, psychological suspense novel. ISBN 0-941483-05-3   8.95

TO THE LIGHTNING by Catherine Ennis. 208 pp. Romantic Lesbian 'Robinson Crusoe' adventure. ISBN 0-941483-06-1   8.95

THE OTHER SIDE OF VENUS by Shirley Verel. 224 pp. Luminous, romantic love story. ISBN 0-941483-07-X   8.95

DREAMS AND SWORDS by Katherine V. Forrest. 192 pp. Romantic, erotic, imaginative stories. ISBN 0-941483-03-7   8.95

MEMORY BOARD by Jane Rule. 336 pp. Memorable novel about an aging Lesbian couple. ISBN 0-941483-02-9   8.95

THE ALWAYS ANONYMOUS BEAST by Lauren Wright Douglas. 224 pp. A Caitlin Reese mystery. First in a series. ISBN 0-941483-04-5   8.95

SEARCHING FOR SPRING by Patricia A. Murphy. 224 pp. Novel about the recovery of love. ISBN 0-941483-00-2   8.95

DUSTY'S QUEEN OF HEARTS DINER by Lee Lynch. 240 pp. Romantic blue-collar novel. ISBN 0-941483-01-0   8.95

PARENTS MATTER by Ann Muller. 240 pp. Parents' relationships with Lesbian daughters and gay sons. ISBN 0-930044-91-6   9.95

THE PEARLS by Shelley Smith. 176 pp. Passion and fun in the Caribbean sun. ISBN 0-930044-93-2   7.95

MAGDALENA by Sarah Aldridge. 352 pp. Epic Lesbian novel set on three continents. ISBN 0-930044-99-1   8.95

THE BLACK AND WHITE OF IT by Ann Allen Shockley. 144 pp. Short stories. ISBN 0-930044-96-7   7.95

SAY JESUS AND COME TO ME by Ann Allen Shockley. 288 pp. Contemporary romance. ISBN 0-930044-98-3   8.95

LOVING HER by Ann Allen Shockley. 192 pp. Romantic love story. ISBN 0-930044-97-5   7.95

MURDER AT THE NIGHTWOOD BAR by Katherine V. Forrest. 240 pp. A Kate Delafield mystery. Second in a series. ISBN 0-930044-92-4   8.95

ZOE'S BOOK by Gail Pass. 224 pp. Passionate, obsessive love story. ISBN 0-930044-95-9   7.95

WINGED DANCER by Camarin Grae. 228 pp. Erotic Lesbian adventure story. ISBN 0-930044-88-6   8.95

PAZ by Camarin Grae. 336 pp. Romantic Lesbian adventurer with the power to change the world. ISBN 0-930044-89-4   8.95

SOUL SNATCHER by Camarin Grae. 224 pp. A puzzle, an adventure, a mystery — Lesbian romance. ISBN 0-930044-90-8   8.95

THE LOVE OF GOOD WOMEN by Isabel Miller. 224 pp.
Long-awaited new novel by the author of the beloved *Patience
and Sarah.*   ISBN 0-930044-81-9   8.95

THE HOUSE AT PELHAM FALLS by Brenda Weathers. 240
pp. Suspenseful Lesbian ghost story.   ISBN 0-930044-79-7   7.95

HOME IN YOUR HANDS by Lee Lynch. 240 pp. More stories
from the author of *Old Dyke Tales.*   ISBN 0-930044-80-0   7.95

EACH HAND A MAP by Anita Skeen. 112 pp. Real-life poems
that touch us all.   ISBN 0-930044-82-7   6.95

SURPLUS by Sylvia Stevenson. 342 pp. A classic early Lesbian
novel.   ISBN 0-930044-78-9   7.95

PEMBROKE PARK by Michelle Martin. 256 pp. Derring-do
and daring romance in Regency England.   ISBN 0-930044-77-0   7.95

THE LONG TRAIL by Penny Hayes. 248 pp. Vivid adventures
of two women in love in the old west.   ISBN 0-930044-76-2   8.95

HORIZON OF THE HEART by Shelley Smith. 192 pp. Hot
romance in summertime New England.   ISBN 0-930044-75-4   7.95

AN EMERGENCE OF GREEN by Katherine V. Forrest. 288
pp. Powerful novel of sexual discovery.   ISBN 0-930044-69-X   8.95

THE LESBIAN PERIODICALS INDEX edited by Claire
Potter. 432 pp. Author & subject index.   ISBN 0-930044-74-6   29.95

DESERT OF THE HEART by Jane Rule. 224 pp. A classic;
basis for the movie *Desert Hearts.*   ISBN 0-930044-73-8   7.95

SPRING FORWARD/FALL BACK by Sheila Ortiz Taylor.
288 pp. Literary novel of timeless love.   ISBN 0-930044-70-3   7.95

FOR KEEPS by Elisabeth Nonas. 144 pp. Contemporary novel
about losing and finding love.   ISBN 0-930044-71-1   7.95

TORCHLIGHT TO VALHALLA by Gale Wilhelm. 128 pp.
Classic novel by a great Lesbian writer.   ISBN 0-930044-68-1   7.95

LESBIAN NUNS: BREAKING SILENCE edited by Rosemary
Curb and Nancy Manahan. 432 pp. Unprecedented autobiographies
of religious life.   ISBN 0-930044-62-2   9.95

THE SWASHBUCKLER by Lee Lynch. 288 pp. Colorful novel
set in Greenwich Village in the sixties.   ISBN 0-930044-66-5   8.95

MISFORTUNE'S FRIEND by Sarah Aldridge. 320 pp. Historical Lesbian novel set on two continents.   ISBN 0-930044-67-3   7.95

A STUDIO OF ONE'S OWN by Ann Stokes. Edited by
Dolores Klaich. 128 pp. Autobiography.   ISBN 0-930044-64-9   7.95

SEX VARIANT WOMEN IN LITERATURE by Jeannette
Howard Foster. 448 pp. Literary history.   ISBN 0-930044-65-7   8.95

A HOT-EYED MODERATE by Jane Rule. 252 pp. Hard-hitting
essays on gay life; writing; art.   ISBN 0-930044-57-6   7.95

FAULTLINE by Sheila Ortiz Taylor. 140 pp. Warm, funny, literate story of a startling family.   ISBN 0-930044-24-X   6.95

THE LESBIAN IN LITERATURE by Barbara Grier. 3d ed. Foreword by Maida Tilchen. 240 pp. Comprehensive bibliography. Literary ratings; rare photos.   ISBN 0-930044-23-1   7.95

ANNA'S COUNTRY by Elizabeth Lang. 208 pp. A woman finds her Lesbian identity.   ISBN 0-930044-19-3   6.95

PRISM by Valerie Taylor. 158 pp. A love affair between two women in their sixties.   ISBN 0-930044-18-5   6.95

BLACK LESBIANS: AN ANNOTATED BIBLIOGRAPHY compiled by J. R. Roberts. Foreword by Barbara Smith. 112 pp. Award-winning bibliography.   ISBN 0-930044-21-5   5.95

THE MARQUISE AND THE NOVICE by Victoria Ramstetter. 108 pp. A Lesbian Gothic novel.   ISBN 0-930044-16-9   4.95

OUTLANDER by Jane Rule. 207 pp. Short stories and essays by one of our finest writers.   ISBN 0-930044-17-7   6.95

ALL TRUE LOVERS by Sarah Aldridge. 292 pp. Romantic novel set in the 1930s and 1940s.   ISBN 0-930044-10-X   7.95

A WOMAN APPEARED TO ME by Renee Vivien. 65 pp. A classic; translated by Jeannette H. Foster.   ISBN 0-930044-06-1   5.00

CYTHEREA'S BREATH by Sarah Aldridge. 240 pp. Romantic novel about women's entrance into medicine.
     ISBN 0-930044-02-9   6.95

TOTTIE by Sarah Aldridge. 181 pp. Lesbian romance in the turmoil of the sixties.   ISBN 0-930044-01-0   6.95

THE LATECOMER by Sarah Aldridge. 107 pp. A delicate love story.   ISBN 0-930044-00-2   5.00

ODD GIRL OUT by Ann Bannon.   ISBN 0-930044-83-5   5.95

I AM A WOMAN by Ann Bannon.   ISBN 0-930044-84-3   5.95

WOMEN IN THE SHADOWS by Ann Bannon.
     ISBN 0-930044-85-1   5.95

JOURNEY TO A WOMAN by Ann Bannon.
     ISBN 0-930044-86-X   5.95

BEEBO BRINKER by Ann Bannon.   ISBN 0-930044-87-8   5.95
    Legendary novels written in the fifties and sixties,
    set in the gay mecca of Greenwich Village.